Terror at the Door

Terror at the Door

A Story of the
Missouri-Kansas Border Conflict
1859-1861

Byron Shutz

The Patrice Press
Tucson, Arizona

Copyright © 1998
Byron C. Shutz

Library of Congress Cataloging-in-Publication Data

Shutz, Byron.
  Terror at the door: a story of the Missouri-Kansas border
conflict 1859-1861 / Byron Shutz
    ISBN 1-880397-25-0
    1. Quantrill, William Clarke, 1837-1865–Fiction.   I. Title.
  PS3569.H868T47   1998
  813'.54–dc21   98-19370
                                                            CIP

The Patrice Press
P. O. Box 85639
Tucson, AZ 85754-5639
1-800-367-9242
books@patricepress.com

Printed in the United States of America

"One man came rapidly to dominate this border warfare: William Clarke Quantrill, chief of the Missouri bushwhackers. For dashing boldness and murderous ferocity his raids into Kansas had no parallel."

—"The Bloodiest Man in American History" by Albert Castel, *American Heritage* Vol. 11, (6).

William Quantrill went to Kansas, "but came back to Jackson County [Missouri] and stayed around these parts until March 1861. He stopped with Marcus Gill, father of Judge Turner A. Gill."

—Andrew Walker, *Kansas City Journal,* May 12, 1888.

"He [Quantrill] stayed a part of the balance of the winter at Mark [Marcus] Gill's. . . . He went with Gill to Texas in the spring of 1861. . . ."

—Letter from Andrew Walker to W. W. Scott, Feb. 3, 1883. Kansas Collection, University Libraries, University of Kansas.

The major characters in this story exist in historical accounts, as do the principal events. Other characters, however, and certain other events, attained reality only in my imagination.

–Byron Shutz
Kansas City, Missouri

1

Mary Jane heard a horse whinny. From the big barn, the stallion whinnied back, pawing the floor and straining against its tether. A man's muttered curse followed the clumping of horses milling about, the jangling of bridles.

Pulling aside the curtain, Mary Jane looked through the distorting pane of window glass. In the yard outside, armed men on horseback moved restlessly back and forth, looking to all sides. Only one rider sat calmly in his saddle, scrutinizing the house. He was dressed in a dark coat, buttoned at the neck, which fell to his knees. A wide-brimmed hat shadowed his face. He held a rifle muzzle up in his right hand, the reins in his left.

Two of the riders moved deliberately to opposite sides of the yard, like men on guard. Pistol butts protruded from leather belts at their waists. Hats pulled low partly concealed their faces. Where the road to the house snaked out of a wooded patch, another rider, rifle held in the crook of his arm, watched the road behind. Eight riders, Mary Jane counted, all strangers.

"Leah, stay in your room!" Mary Jane shouted up the stairway to her sixteen-year-old daughter, and then took each of the two younger children firmly by hand, hurrying them into the pantry.

"Millie," she whispered to the Negro nursemaid, "try to keep them quiet. Give them something to play with."

Millie, her eyes wide with fear, picked up the youngest and held her close, wrapping her chubby arms around her. The next youngest child, hugging a doll, clung to Millie's dress, her face bewildered.

Mary Jane, a small woman with precise features, black hair pulled back, quickly closed the door. She pressed her trembling hands against her brown patterned full-length dress, and stepped into the front room.

A man's voice rang out, authoritative and brusque, sounding alarmingly close, as if he were already inside the house.

"Mrs. Gill, we don't want to harm you or your children, but"–he paused ominously–"we know your husband's in Westport, and won't be back 'til tomorrow."

Mary Jane gasped. How could he know that Marcus had gone with their son and the foreman to take the hogs to market?

"We're hungry, ma'am. We'd like you to cook up something for us to eat." When Mary Jane didn't answer, he called out again, "See here, ma'am, open the door. Otherwise we'll have to force our way in. You don't want that, do you? I'll leave my men outside, if that'll make you feel any better."

Her husband's warning before he had left for Westport raced through her mind. Be careful, he'd said, and watch out for strangers. Just a few weeks ago, anti-slavery guerrillas from Kansas Territory had raided a farm near Harrisonville. They terrorized the family and stole horses. Neighbors said that the guerrillas threatened to take the slaves, too, to set free them free, but gathered up so much loot that they hastily rode off, leaving the slaves behind.

Mary Jane cracked the door and looked out. The man staring at her from the saddle of his horse loomed black against the sky. The horse's chest and flanks were flaked with sweat. The ground, vulnerable from a hard rain, was gouged by hoof marks.

"Who are you, " Mary Jane asked, struggling to keep her voice steady. "What do you want?"

"Like I said, ma'am, we'd just like some dinner. We've covered a lot of territory since we left home, and haven't eaten since last evening."

As a Southerner, Mary Jane's instinct was to offer hospitality, but these men were not travelers on the road. "Well, I don't know," she said, hoping to put them off. "We've just had our breakfast. I don't think–"

"And I don't want to be rude, ma'am," he interrupted, "but we don't plan on looking anywhere else."

He thrust his rifle through a ring fastened to the saddle horn, and slid to the ground. Handing the reins off to another rider, he approached the house.

"I'm coming in, Mrs. Gill. My men will wait outside until you've got dinner ready." To the rider nearest him, he said in a low voice, "Put two men at the door. We don't want any surprises."

With no other choice, Mary Jane opened the door wider, and fell back into the room. Leah, who had slipped down the stairs despite her mother's warning, passed quickly behind her and went to the pantry to help Millie with the younger children.

The stranger removed his hat, ducked his head, and stepped through the door. He was middle-aged and had long hair and a beard the color of slate. Where his hat brim had pressed against his head, the hair was matted. Dirt rings formed by sweat, now dried, circled his throat above the collar of the black scarf knotted above his coat. He smelled of horses, sweat, and woodsmoke.

"Anybody else in the house? Where are your children?" Suspiciously, he looked up the stairway, then toward the closed door into the pantry, and beyond that, the opening that led into the kitchen.

"They're in the pantry, with Millie." Her voice was matter-of-fact. They were no threat to him, she said to herself, so there was no cause for him to harm them.

"She can look after them while you fix us up something?"

Mary Jane ignored the question, struggling to keep her face calm.

"You didn't answer my first question," he said. "Anybody else in the house?"

Mary Jane shook her head. "No. Just my oldest daughter, Leah. She's with the younger children, back there."

Then she quickly added, "She'll be helping me in the kitchen, since I guess you'll be staying."

"My name's—" He barely hesitated. "Slater, Mrs. Gill. Slater."

Mary Jane sensed the name was false.

He then strode toward the pantry, dried mud caked on the sides of his boots flaking onto the polished floor. Standing to one side of the door, his hand on the butt of the revolver in his belt, he pushed it open. Satisfied with what he saw, he turned and bounded up the stairway two steps at a time, the revolver now in his hand. The forceful sound of his boots striking the wood boards of the floor as he went from one room to the next were a jarring intrusion.

Returning, Slater went to the open front door of the house, and motioned to a man who had been waiting to come inside.

"But you said–," Mary Jane called out. "You said that your men–" By then, Slater had disappeared outside.

The man who entered was short and bony, pale, and nearly bald. A distorted grin bared his twisted teeth, yellowed by tobacco juice. He carried a chicken in each grimy hand, head cleaved from the neck, white carcasses splashed with blood.

Holding up the chickens, he said, "Howdy, ma'am. Thought I'd help out with dinner. Caught these two out back while you and him were jawboning. I'll take 'em to the kitchen and clean 'em for you, ma'am." He snickered, still beaming.

Repulsed and infuriated, Mary Jane turned away, hiding her anger, and led him toward the kitchen.

Minutes later, another man sauntered through the front door. Stocky, hat low over his eyes, with matted yellowish hair to his collar, he was dressed like a farmer. He appeared to be about Slater's age. Looking carefully about the well-furnished room, he saw what he was searching for. He walked over to a large trunk on the floor against one wall. A brocaded cloth in motifs of rich red, gilt yellow, and blue, lay across the top. The man took off the cloth, crumpling it in his hands, and watched, fascinated, when the fabric, as if alive, regained its unwrinkled appearance. He chuckled, and stuffed the cloth into a large pocket on the side of his coat.

The trunk now revealed to him was finely made, no ordinary piece, and bearing no sign of abuse incurred by being bounced about in a wagon. It was constructed of belting leather, stretched on a sturdy frame of oak. Dyed the color of mahogany, the leather was polished into dark reflective surfaces. Burnished brass clasps embellished the front.

The man reached down, turned the key in each of the locks, undid the clasps, and lifted up the lid. Rummaging through table linens and comforters, he irritably pulled them out and tossed them on the floor. Next came account books, land abstracts, and bulky ledgers. Recorded in them by seasons of the year were the minutiae of farming, such as seed bought and planted, weather, crop yields, calves born, and slaves purchased and sold. He piled all these carelessly on the floor, to get them out of the way.

Among the remaining items at the bottom of the trunk he saw a substantial-looking box, a small chest. Lacquered-wood surfaces gleamed with light, and leather trimmed the edges. He leaned down into the trunk, grasped the box with both hands, grunted, lifted it up, and because of its weight, set it down carefully on the table.

"Got it," he muttered to himself with obvious satisfaction, and looked as if he would call out to Slater, but didn't. Opening the lid of the chest, he took out a handful of silver tableware. He selected an ornate silver table knife which he held up to the window light, admiring the strange filigree-like decoration.

"Put those back!" Leah stood in the door to the pantry, arms stiff at her side, fists tight. "Those aren't yours. You put them right back," she demanded.

Startled, he looked at her, his eyes widening in surprise.

"I mean it," she said. "What do you mean, getting into our things?"

The man shrugged. "Now, now, little lady, no need for you to get all upset," he said, as if calming a small child.

"But they belonged to my grandmother. We brought them with us, from Kentucky. They're very valuable."

Unperturbed, the man dropped the silver pieces into a cloth pouch hanging from a strap at his shoulder. "I know that, ma'am, that's why I'm taking them. And that ain't all you brought with you, is it?" the man added. "You also brung slaves, didn't you? Slaves, human beings you'd bought. That you own. Own! You shouldn't have done that, bringing slaves here."

He took a step toward Leah, his arms rising as if he might shake her by the shoulders. "We don't want slaves in these parts. We don't like slavery. We don't like Southerners, neither."

"Who are you to tell us what we should do?" Leah retorted, not moving, her head up.

He stopped, looked at her hard, started to speak, them shrugged and turned his back. He dumped the rest of the silver into the pouch, and went outside, not looking back.

Leah, tears in her eyes, fled to the kitchen.

She had only just left when yet another man came into the room, blinking his eyes in the subdued light, his face smudged with road dust. About twenty, he was thin and hollow-eyed, with straight, coffee-colored hair. Despite several days growth of beard and an untidy look, he wore a fine bleached-linen shirt, a dark-red neckerchief around his neck, a woolen vest trimmed in black, and a narrow felt hat with a purple ribbon wrapped round the crown.

Seeing the pantry door standing open, he sauntered over and looked inside. "Where's the whiskey kept?" he asked. Millie, clutching the two-year-old, kept her eyes downcast.

The boy's sisters, playing on the floor, gazed up at the stranger.

Shrugging, the man began noisily opening cabinets along one wall. When he found the whiskey, he opened one of the bottles, took a long drink, then grasped two other bottles in his left hand. Walking to the front door, he handed the bottles to one of the men standing just outside. "Here you are, boys. Pass it around. Plenty more inside."

The whiskey bottle hanging from one hand, he sauntered around the room. He picked up a small glass paperweight lying on a table, held it up to his eye, squinted through the glass at other objects in the room, then dropped it into his jacket pocket. A child's walnut rocking chair sat next to a spindle-backed armchair pulled back from a writing table. The intruder stepped over to the child's chair, and with the toe of his boot nudged the edge of the seat, causing the chair to bob back and forth. The rockers hitting against the uneven floor planks made a far-away hollow sound.

Restlessly, the man wandered over to an upholstered wing chair near the great hearth where unfinished needlepoint in a floral design, left there by Mary Jane the night before, lay on the seat of the chair. He picked up the needlepoint, scrutinized the intricate needlework, but not knowing what to make of it, put it back where it had been.

The man then saw a bulky family Bible, the size of three ordinary books, bound in leather and fastened with a metal hasp, lying atop a chest of drawers. Impatient, he opened it and leafed through the first few pages, squinting at handwritten recordings in brown ink of births, deaths, and marriages. He read a few entries, mouthing the names, and took another drink of whiskey, then shut the book and gazed around the rest of the room.

The rich odor of food cooking and sounds of activity came from the kitchen. He went to the open door and leaned against the door jamb, watching the women preparing the meal. The room was warm from the wood fire in the large iron range. Mary Jane stood at the stove, turning pieces of chicken frying in an iron pan, a white apron covering the front of her dress. A woman slave, called in by Mary Jane to help out, sat at a table, peeling potatoes. A pot of green beans simmered on the back of the range. A black skillet with dark-brown gravy sat warming near the edge. No one spoke.

Leah stood at a table, cutting pies baked earlier that morning, just removed from the oven. Her face was flushed from the heat, her long dark hair pulled back and tied loosely with a bright ribbon. She placed the pie slices on a serving plate, her agile hands moving adeptly as she worked. The light-yellow blouse she wore was open at the neck, the top two buttons unfastened, the sleeves pushed above the elbows. Perspiration beaded her brow, and her slender neck was moist.

The man remained in the doorway, slouching, and stared at Leah. She seemed preoccupied with her task, and did not look back at him, although her body tensed under his scrutiny.

"My name's Ephraim," he said. Leah said nothing, ducking her head slightly.

"When do you expect you'll be ready so we can eat? I'm mighty hungry."

Without looking up, Mary Jane curtly replied, "We'll come tell you."

Ephriam grunted, but kept his eyes on Leah. She skillfully sliced wedges of bright-red tomatoes on a wood chopping board and arranged them in circles on a platter.

"I live on a farm, too," he said. "West of here, quite a ways. Fact is, took most of the night to get here."

His eyes traveled from her long hair, down her youthful figure, and back to the delicate profile of her face. Leah kept her eyes down.

Ignored, Ephriam looked resentful. Petulance crept into the corners of his mouth. Finally, hitching up his trousers, he took another drink of whiskey, shivered in spite of the heat, and turned away. Passing the stairway, he stopped. No one else was in the room. He looked up toward the second floor, and began climbing the stairs, treading softly, muffling the sound of his boots.

In the kitchen, Mary Jane picked up a plate of food scraps and stepped to the back door to throw them out for the cats. Her eyes widened in surprise at what she saw. Three of the strangers were leading a half-dozen horses out of the corral with rope bridles, headed toward the yard in front of the house. Another man was harnessing two of her husband's horses to one of the box wagons that Marcus kept in a covered shed. The wagon had been loaded with saddles, harnesses, farming tools, and large bags of grain from the barn.

Furious, she put down the pan and hurried into the front room. Slater leaned back in a rocking chair, one leg crossed over the other, smoking a cigar. Her husband's humidor, the cover standing open, sat on the table next to him.

"Mr. Slater, you've got to stop your men," she hurled at him. "They're stealing our horses. They're taking things out of the barn that don't belong to them. You have no right to do that."

Slater puffed serenely on the cigar, returning the stare with eyes partly closed against the smoke. "You just go on back to your kitchen, Mrs. Gill. My men are doing what they came to do."

"But we haven't done anything to you. I don't even—"

"Well, I'll tell you, Mrs. Gill," he broke in, suddenly angry, "me and my men just as soon you and your husband and other Southerners like you would pack up and take your slaves with you back to where you came from. We don't like your ways, and we're not going to tolerate slavery. Not in Vermont, where I come from, not in Missouri, not anywhere."

He got up from the chair, his head nearly brushing the ceiling. "People like you bring slaves and settle down right close to us. We do our own farming. We don't buy slaves." Brown's face was taut, his eyes almost closed. "If we need more help, we hire it. We don't go buy ourselves another slave. What you do is disgusting, immoral. It's abominable. In fact, I—"

From the floor above, from Leah's room, they heard a man's voice singing drunkenly, and sounds of commotion. Mary Jane spun around, and hurried up the stairs. Brown followed at a deliberate pace.

When they reached the bedroom door, they saw Ephriam jumping up and down on Leah's bed, her clothes underfoot, scattered across the bed and on the floor nearby. Leah's room was never cluttered, yet drawers to a dresser now stood open, and one drawer, completely pulled out, lay empty on the floor. The partly-empty whiskey bottle was next to it.

When he saw Slater, Ephriam stopped jumping, and sheepishly climbed down off the bed. "Just having a little fun," he said. "Ain't done nobody no harm." He sidled past them, and went down the stairs, stumbling when he got near the bottom.

Leah came out of the kitchen. She saw the expression on her mother's face as she descended the stairs, but when Mary Jane put her finger to her lips, Leah only said, "We're ready to feed them."

Slater, a thin smile on his face, followed Ephriam out the door.

For Mary Jane and Leah, waiting in the kitchen, the meal seemed endless. All the men except Slater behaved as if they were at a tavern. They passed around another bottle of whiskey from the cabinet while they ate hungrily, told stories, laughed, and boasted about the loot outside in the box wagon, the money they'd get for those fine horses. The pale-skinned, almost bald man who had carried in the headless chickens, carried plates of food outside to the men who remained on guard.

Slater was silent, absorbed in his eating. Mary Jane thought him an odd man: dangerous and determined, yet probably educated, principled in his own way. She had never known anyone from New England. The depth of his repulsion at slavery puzzled her. How could someone of apparent moral substance resort to such violence, force his way into her home, rob, intimidate, all in the name of protesting against slavery? The fact that such a man could conduct himself in this way frightened her even more, because she recognized that without boundaries, without restraints, anything could happen.

When the men had finished eating the slices of pie served on a platter in the middle of the table, all except Slater got up and left the house. He pushed away from the table, leaned back in his chair, and lighted a second cigar, as relaxed as if he were a guest about to have a pleasant conversation with his hostess.

Mary Jane began carrying dishes out to the kitchen.

"One more thing, Mrs. Gill," Slater said. "Your husband's got to have some cash hidden somewhere. He's a wealthy man. I want you to show me where it is."

Mary Jane stopped, and looked directly at him. "Haven't you stolen enough? Caused us enough trouble?"

Slater chuckled. "Well, now, we'd have taken more, but we figure we've already got about as much as we can carry." He held the cigar between his thumb and forefinger, his elbow resting on the arm of the chair, and stared at her, his face blank. "Now, then, where's the money hidden?"

"I don't know. There isn't any."

Slater gazed at her thoughtfully, puffing on the cigar. "Your daughter Leah's a mighty pretty young woman, Mrs. Gill. Ephriam seems right taken with her." With a finger he tapped the cigar, dropping the ash onto the floor. "We don't have to leave right away, you know. We've got time."

Mary Jane could hardly speak; her voice was a whisper. "How dare you?"

Slater just stared. The cigar smoke, transparent, white, drifted above him.

"Well?" he asked again. "Where's the money?"

"My husband took it with him. To pay cash for things he needs."

"You don't have any other money in the house?" Slater watched her closely.

"No."

"Are you quite sure, Mrs. Gill? Like I said, we're in no hurry to leave such fine hospitality." Slater narrowed his eyes against the smoke. "I'm real sure Ephriam would be willing to leave whatever he's doing right at this moment and go back upstairs where he was having himself a fine time."

Mary Jane set the dishes back on the table, and went into the front room. Slater followed. She opened the family Bible, and found 1st Corinthians. Compressed flat between the pages of parchment-like paper were several hundred-dollar bills.

"This is all there is. I put it there myself. For anything unexpected." She handed the money to Slater.

"Thank you, ma'am. That was very wise of you." He tucked the money inside his coat. "We'll be leaving, now." He turned and left the house.

Trembling, one hand clenched at her mouth, Mary Jane stood for a moment at the front window, watching the men ride off. The stolen horses, tethered by ropes to their captors, trotted along, complacent. She turned and gazed about the room. The clotted mud from Slater's boots dirtied her floor. She gazed at the ravaged trunk, the empty silver chest, the table linens and comforters dumped on the muddied floor. These men had defiled the air, and violated her house, sullied it with their coarse humor, their greed, the crude threats.

They were nothing more than thieves hiding behind abolitionist views, not lawful men like her husband. Marcus believed in lawfulness; it was integral to his character. He would never do what they had done, even to maintain slavery. These men didn't care about freeing slaves; instead, they had desecrated her house. Their purpose, she knew, was to steal property to enrich themselves, and to intimidate women, to frighten them.

The raiders had threatened her family, and might have done much worse. Still quivering from the violent confrontation with Slater, she could not rid her mind of the image that Leah might have been brutally harmed had she not divulged where the money was hidden. The rawness of the fear humiliated her, made her feel weak, and the sense of weakness angered her.

Leah's sudden shriek propelled Mary Jane toward the kitchen. Leah and the slaves stood at the open back door, looking toward the wagon shed. Smoke tumbled above the roof, and flames erupted from the wide door and curled about the window frames.

The raiders had set the wagon shed on fire before they rode off.

2

A few weeks later, in the crisp October air, Marcus Gill rode his quarter horse across fields cut clean of corn stalks. Dry, twisted fragments of stalks and veined leaves lying on the ground spoke back to the horse and rider as they passed.

Marcus was a solid-looking man of medium height, with black hair and beard beginning to gray, although he was not yet fifty. His eyes, steady and light gray in color, had flecks of ice green. In conversation, he could appear when listening to be standing back, as if watching from a distance, his gaze remote and his face lacking expression. At times, he would tilt his head back slightly, and to one side, as if contemplating the speaker. He seemed both formidable and detached. Yet, when moved by a guileless question from one of his young children, or by an affectionate gesture from Mary Jane, his face opened with warmth, his eyes momentarily glistening with pleasure.

Marcus sat his horse with the ease gained when a boy in Kentucky. His hands held the reins as lightly as, when a child playing in the barn, he would pick up a swallow's egg from a fallen nest. His father had hoisted the three-year-old Marcus and placed him bareback astride a placid mare. His father threaded the boy's fingers around the reins so that he could hold them in his own uncertain hands; then continued talking quietly as he led the mare in a wide circle slowly around the barn lot, guiding her with the bit. When the boy was five, his father gave permission for Marcus to ride the mare alone, within a small fenced pasture next to the barn. Marcus did not know that his father had instructed Jim, the slave who would saddle the mare, to keep an eye on his son from the barn door as long as the boy rode, and made Jim accountable for the boy's safety.

But now, as his horse loped across the fields, Marcus thought again about Slater and the band of men who had been with him. He knew it could have been even worse. Other raiders from Kansas Territory, in moments of anger or drunkenness, or if they met even unarmed resistance, had shot and killed farmers and adult sons with no provocation. Wives and daughters were intimidated and terrorized, a part of the strategy to drive slave-owning farmers out of the state.

Why such violence? Stealing of slaves by anti-slavery forces was increasing. Farmers in Kansas territory near Lawrence, even townspeople with abolitionist views, sheltered fleeing slaves until they could be passed along to other sympathizers and finally reach freedom in the north. Raiders hoped that slave-owning farmers in Missouri would feel compelled to flee, taking their families farther south, out of the state. But why, Marcus thought, why should he yield to such threats? Owning slaves was lawful. He had bought them. They were his property.

When Marcus came to Missouri with his family, he assembled a thousand acres of land in Jackson County bordering the Kansas Territory. Virgin land, it had never been cultivated. He arrived confident that he could transform this land into a richly productive farm of row crops and livestock for which there would be an expanding market.

Magnificent stands of mature trees covered a part of the property. They provided logs and lumber to construct the buildings he would need. A creek for watering livestock ran through the land. Well water, cold and pure, was within reach not far below the surface. The gentler slopes of the rolling land Marcus could cultivate with row crops; the sharper hills would remain in pasture, fenced with wood rail.

His slaves, more than twenty of them brought from Kentucky, were the sinew, the muscle of this transfiguration. They felled the trees with axes, hacking the undergrowth into brush piles set afire to burn. The smoke twisted upward into the sky, the roiling blaze forcing laborers to stand back. Slaves broke the sod with teams of mules dragging V-shaped glinting blades, turning the ground, burying the thick prairie grasses which would soon decay under dark waves of earth. Then smaller blades, set close like soldiers in rank, broke up the solid clods, so that at last the seed could be planted.

Other slaves cut down and trimmed tree trunks into logs to build the big main house and the slave cabins. Marcus set up a sawmill, powered by water from the creek, flush with spring rains, to make wood boards for the barns, hog sheds, chicken coops, and wagon sheds.

Nearby, the village of New Santa Fe flourished. The hollow sound of hammer blows driving nails into freshly sawed lumber echoed everywhere. On the town's one business street, new settlers passed by with little notice, there were so many. A general store offered essential supplies. At the edge of town, a blacksmith shoed horses and made iron door latches, hinges, nails, and tools. A post office, church, and a stable shared one side of the dusty street which quickly turned into ankle-deep mud when spring rains came. Ten miles to the north, the town of Westport published a weekly newspaper, four folded sheets which left smudges of printer's ink on a reader's hands.

But abolitionists in Kansas Territory, vehemently opposed to slavery, had begun making trouble about 1854, the year Marcus and his family arrived. County sheriffs lacked enough men to find and prosecute the lawless. The ranks of federal troops in the county were slim; but worse, they did not intercede.

The countryside was too vast, the raiders too quick, for enforcement of federal and state laws protecting slave owners and other victims of random violence. Marcus knew he was not guilty of any crime, yet those who thought slavery wrong repeatedly threatened him and other farmers. He felt that these attackers envied the wealth that slavery engendered, and feared that slavery might move westward, unabated, into Kansas Territory.

Marcus felt beleaguered. Like criminals, raiders cloaked their identity, hiding behind faces unrecognized and names unknown. Slavery was lawful, yet these men were not. They violated a lawful act, the practice of slavery, to justify their crimes.

Marcus looked about him as he rode across the fields. With harvest over, his spirits lightened. He saw grain bins straining under burdens of corn. Shoots of yellow hay projected between slats in haylofts stacked to the eves. Meadowlarks whistled from the pastures, and swallows dipped and soared near the roofs of the big barns. The rich soil rested until next spring, when the plow blades would once again cut crisply, turning the glistening, fecund earth to face the sun.

Riding across his land, Marcus scanned the horizon from time to time for signs of strangers on horseback. The bold sun warming his back masked the pressing apprehension, the fear that he avoided discussing openly with Mary Jane. When he began wearing a revolver heavy in the leather holster at his waist, she did not ask why. Away from the house any distance, he also carried a rifle slung across the saddle, or wore it on his back, secured by a strap over his shoulder and across his chest.

Marcus stopped to open a gate, leaning down from his saddle to lift the latch. The mare dropped her head, straining against the reins to graze on pasture grass, still a lush, cool green, bright with dew. He pulled firmly on the bridle reins to raise her head.

Looking up, he saw against the skyline a solitary figure on horseback approaching the house from the west, from Kansas Territory. He was expecting no one. His son Turner, seventeen, had left earlier that morning for New Santa Fe to pick up the mail. This rider was coming from the opposite direction, and would reach his house before Marcus could be there.

With a slight pressure of the reins against her neck, Marcus quickly turned the mare and at a gallop followed a narrow cattle path back toward the house. When he reached the corral, he handed the reins to the stable boy and saw another leading Turner's horse into the barn. Near the house, the stranger's mount was already tied at the rail.

His hand on the revolver at his waist, Marcus cautiously stepped inside the house. In the parlor Turner was talking to a man in his early twenties. At the sound of Marcus's boots on the wood planking, they turned toward him. The stranger held loosely in his hands a dark, low-crown felt hat.

"Father, this is Will Quantrill, the schoolteacher I told you about."

Quantrill stepped forward to shake hands. "Pleased to meet you, Colonel Gill."

The man was slender, about the same height as Marcus. He looked agile, Marcus thought, and supple, like a willow branch that springs back when one's grasp is released. Marcus also sensed the hard muscles beneath the slack, open-necked shirt the younger man wore. Quantrill's gaze, curious and confident, met Marcus Gill's.

"Yes, Turner told me about you," Marcus said. "Says you're a right good teacher. Over at Stanton." Marcus took off his coat, laid it across the back of a chair. "But you're from back East, I hear. Where 'bouts?"

"Ohio. Came west two years ago. Went to Utah for a spell in spring of last year."

Marcus gestured toward a chair. "What brought you to Missouri?"

His lean guest had a sunburned, slightly boyish face, unperturbed blue eyes, and hair the color of wheat chaff, slicked down on each side.

"You may know Henry Chiles," Will replied. "Has a place back toward Westport. Hired me as a bullwhacker when he took fifty wagons of freight to Salt Lake for Russell-Majors."

He looked carefully at Marcus for a reaction.

In fact, Marcus remembered that one day in town not long ago, Henry Chiles had complained about the man when telling Marcus about the trip to Utah. Chiles, who had been wagon boss on the trip west, was contemptuous of Quantrill's rambunctious behavior, yet grudgingly admitted he was a fine horseman and an excellent shot when hunting game to feed the wagon crew. Chiles also said that one of these days Quantrill would get himself into serious trouble. Daring, disdainful of authority, that kind of man usually did.

Turner spoke eagerly to his father. "You've said that with me leaving soon for the university, you'd like to have another man on the place. Will would be mighty good for you to have around, if there was trouble. He's the best shot I've ever seen."

Marcus thought for a moment. Despite Chiles's criticism, Marcus liked his guest's assurance, his easy composure.

"What are your plans, Mr. Quantrill?"

"Well, sir, I'll be teaching school 'til spring."

"Where are you staying?"

"Mr. Bennings has been putting me up. His place is a mite far from school, though, compared to what you are here."

Marcus knew old man Bennings, a farmer in the Kansas Territory. Unlike many, he was friendly toward Missourians, a pro-slavery man. Marcus probed further. "Coming from back east, how do you feel about Kansas Territory going free-state? Barring slavery. There're some who hold firmly to that idea."

"Well, I figure a man's entitled to his property, including slaves. Law says he can own them. Besides, I'm told settlers in the Territory will have a choice whether it'll be free or slave, but I hope they go slave. Just makes sense, Missouri already having slaves."

Without comment, Marcus turned to his son. "Turner, Mr. Quantrill might like a little of that whiskey we brought from Kentucky last trip I made. Fetch some glasses."

Quantrill sat back in his chair, relaxed. "Turner said you were a colonel in the militia in Kentucky, before you came out to Missouri. I suspect you don't think much of those ruffians coming over from Kansas and causing a lot of trouble."

Marcus said nothing.

"Well, sir," Quantrill plunged ahead, "I've seen what those Jayhawkers do, and I can tell you, it just isn't right. They say they're against slavery, but I'm inclined to think they're mostly interested in raising hell and stealing another man's property." He watched Marcus closely for any reaction. "Abolitionists, men like Lane and Montgomery, they don't like folks from the South, folks who've got slaves. They've got no tolerance for that."

Turner returned from the pantry and set the bottle and glasses down on a table. Marcus poured the whiskey, handed a glass to Quantrill, and raised his glass in the gesture of a salute.

"Thank you, sir." Quantrill downed the liquor, and sat with one leg crossed casually over the other, his slender fingers playing with the empty glass.

Marcus asked, "Have you had a part in any of the fighting? Giving the raiders a bad time when they show up?"

"Haven't exactly had much of a chance since I got back from Utah, but I've been thinking about maybe giving some of the folks around here a hand, if they need it."

Will grinned, then threw out, "Man got in my way, out in

Utah, so I had to kill him. I'm not fearful of doing what needs to be done. Fact is, I'm not much afraid of anything."

Marcus didn't like Quantrill's boasting, and guessed he might be lying about the killing, trying to impress. Quantrill struck Marcus as a young man anxious for praise. But Marcus also recognized that such a man could be useful, if he hired Quantrill to help protect his family. He decided to take the chance.

"Like I said, Will's a real good shot," Turner offered. "I once saw him put a bullet hole though a big sow's ear from about ten yards. That old sow let out a squeal and ran around the pen a couple times, but didn't hurt her at all." Turner laughed, and his father smiled. Will looked pleased.

Turner soon left for his first year at the university, halfway across the state. A few days later, Will Quantrill moved into a small, bare-floored room with a low ceiling in the attic of Marcus Gill's house. The room contained only a rope bed, wood chair, clothes tree, coal oil lamp, a mid-size trunk for storage, and chamber pot. For room, board, and a little money, he would be another man with a gun, if needed, when night darkened the roads from the west.

Schooldays, Will was up and gone by daybreak, quietly slipping out on horseback to arrive early at the simple frame building near Stanton. Winter came early that year, bringing snow, then two days of melting, followed by cold and more snow. There was but one schoolroom, almost square, with rough-sawn floor, a window on each of two sides, narrow entrance door, and exposed rafters above which the roof quickly peaked. Will would start the wood fire in the hulking iron stove, sweep the floor, and then wait for his students of varied ages to arrive on horseback or by foot.

At the end of the school day, he liked to linger for a time, reading or planning the next day's lesson. One afternoon, he began a letter to his widowed mother in Ohio.

> Stanton, Kansas Terri.
>
> My dear Mother
>   I again seat myself down to pen you a few lines, hoping they may cheer you in a measure, and if so, it is all I can do at this time. . . .
>   In my last letter I said we have had quite fine weather here, but I can now look out of the window at my school-house and see every thing clad in snow & ice, which was put on but last night, and now seems to hold every thing in its cold embrace, indeed so sudden has been the change that it seems not only to have caught the forest & prairie napping in the sunshine but the people also, for I feel it myself and seem to shudder when I look out upon the snow covered ground & hear the cold wind whistle around & through the forest. . . .

Will laid down his pen, stood up from the desk, and walked over to a window where he stood for a moment, pensive. Cold air breached the glass, chilling his face as he watched the wind churn the dry snow into cone-shaped drifts against the fence posts. He then went back to his writing.

> You have undoubtedly heard of the wrongs committed in this territory by the southern people or pro-slavery party, but when one once knows the facts they can easily see that it has been the opposite party that have been the main mov-ers in the troubles & by far the most lawless set of people in the country. They all sympathize for old J. Brown who should have been hanged years ago, indeed hanging was too good for him. May I never see a more contemptible people than those who sympathize with him. A murderer and a robber made a martyr of, just think of it.

Abruptly, Will angrily threw down his pen and stood up, jarring the small desk. He felt a rush of anger toward all abolitionists, a swelling up of frustration. He longed to strike out, to take action, to be someone.

In the ebbing light of dusk and the silence of nightfall, Will returned to the Marcus Gill farm, cold, hungry, and despondent, and climbed the steps to his room in the attic.

3

In early December, Marcus accepted an invitation from a friend who worked actively for pro-slavery forces in the Kansas Territory to hear a man named Lincoln, a lawyer from Illinois, speak at Leavenworth, just inside the Kansas Territory. Marcus arranged to spend the night at Mansion House, where Lincoln, visiting the Territory early in his bid for the Republican presidential nomination, was staying.

Abolition of slavery was gaining support, Marcus knew, in the newly formed Republican Party. Newspapers in St. Louis, available three days later in Westport, reported the stories. Marcus was a Democrat, and Democrats in the South were traditionally pro-slavery. He was curious to learn what this man from Illinois, also born in Kentucky, but already known for anti-slavery pronouncements, had to say about the right of slave owners like himself to keep their slaves. In the face of rising public outcries in the north and northeast against slavery, would Lincoln, speaking from a platform on the edge of a slave state, now reassert the right to keep slaves in order to accommodate a more Southern audience?

Newspapers reported that Lincoln might be content just to stem the expansion of slavery into western territories. He had even declared that if voters would agree with him to commit the nation to equality, to the actual practice of freedom for all men, then the institution of slavery could continue in those states where slavery already existed until it eventually died out of its own accord. Marcus favored this solution; it seemed to him a practical and realistic compromise.

On Saturday evening, Marcus and his friend went early to Stockton's Hall, where Lincoln would appear. Gas-flamed light fixtures high on the walls of the room cast a sputtering, raw light. Tobacco smoke hovered above the heads of those already seated. Standing room at the back of the hall was crowded with men jostling for a better view. Those who couldn't get in collected at the doors where they might catch a glimpse of the would-be candidate for president.

Almost without notice, Lincoln entered the back of the hall and started down a side aisle, stopping to shake a stranger's hand or grasp a well-wisher by the shoulder. Marcus was struck by the gaunt angularity of the man. A head taller than most, Lincoln's beardless cheeks were sunken in the sallow face, the black hair disarranged. He looked austere, not at all like a politician, yet took his time, looking full in the eyes each man he greeted.

On the unadorned stage were two spindle-backed chairs. Lincoln mounted the stairs awkwardly and sat down on one of the chairs, noticeably too small for him. He gazed out at the assemblage from deep-set eyes, his knees apart and thrust high by the low seat, legs stiffly vertical like sticks poked in the ground. Marcus thought Lincoln resembled a great grass-hopper, sitting there stolidly in the chair, and smiled slightly in amusement.

Less than respectful, the crowd continued talking among themselves until the man who would introduce Lincoln got up and called for order. After an effusive introduction, he gave Lincoln the floor.

Marcus watched curiously as Lincoln carefully arose and stepped forward. His tall frame diminished the fragile-looking lectern. As he began speaking, Lincoln seemed inelegant and forbidding, but gradually his voice became strong and firm, resonating in an unexpectedly high pitch throughout the room. Marcus listened intently.

Lincoln knew that there were pro-slavery listeners in the audience. Before long he spoke directly to them.

"You are for the Union; and you greatly fear the success of the Republicans would destroy the Union. Why?"

Lincoln paused, and looked about the room. "Your own statement of it is, that if the Republicans elect a president, you won't stand for it. You will break up the Union." Abolishing slavery was a plank in the Republican platform. Because of that, some derisively called the party "the black Republicans." Marcus thought it an apt description.

The audience hushed as Lincoln challenged the upturned faces. "That will be your act, not ours," he admonished. "To justify it you must show that our policy gives you just cause for such desperate action. Can you do that?"

Marcus fully knew, as did the cagey Lincoln, that slave owners were trapped in a dilemma. On one hand, the Constitution of the United States gave the right to own slaves. But outside the South, this fact flew in the face of public opinion growing vigorously against slavery. How can it be said, newspaper editors who opposed slavery strongly argued, that all men are equal, as stated in the Bill of Rights, yet black men, women, and children are still enslaved? How can a nation founded on freedom, they wrote, condone slavery?

But Marcus believed that slaves are property, like horses, mules, and other work animals. He bought them to perform certain tasks, mostly to work in the fields, once the land had been cleared. Women slaves tilled the large garden, others made clothes or worked in the house.

Marcus acknowledged that pro-slavery members of Congress had for years skillfully used the threat of secession to gain legislation reinforcing slavery. He had supported such efforts. Lincoln, who also knew of the maneuverings, now dealt with that threat sternly.

"Do you really think," he said vigorously, "that you are justified to break up the government rather than have it administered by President Washington and other good and great men who made it and first administered it?" Again silence. Marcus felt uneasy, and looked at others around him to determine their reaction.

"If you do," Lincoln continued, unrelenting, "you are very unreasonable; and men who are more reasonable cannot and will not submit to you."

The blunt statement dismayed Marcus. How, he thought to himself, can he operate his farm without slaves? He'd spent hard cash money for his slaves, as much as fifteen hundred dollars for a field hand. That's more than he'd pay for fifty acres of good land. Who would repay him, he wondered, for the money he'd invested in slaves, if forced to free them?

Yet, Lincoln the candidate was making it clear that, if

elected president, he would not accept slavery. Neither would he tolerate the threat of secession by those who insisted on slavery. Marcus was alarmed. How could the man be so uncompromising?

Lincoln's long black coat hung loosely on his skeletal frame. He took a few steps forward, almost to the edge of the platform. "If we shall constitutionally elect a president," he averred forcefully, "it will be our duty to see that you submit." He paused, adding, "Old John Brown has just been executed for treason against the state."

Murmurs swept through the crowd. They knew about Osawatomie and Harper's Ferry.

"We cannot object to his execution," Lincoln quickly followed, "even though he agreed with us in thinking slavery wrong. That cannot excuse violence, bloodshed, and treason. It could avail him nothing that he might think himself right."

Marcus agreed. Vindictive and ruthless, John Brown had shot down those who owned slaves. He had been a murderer, acting outside the law.

The candidate was unflinching. "So if constitutionally we Republicans elect a president, and therefore you undertake to destroy the Union, it will be our duty to deal with you as Old John Brown has been dealt with."

But what have we done wrong? Marcus wondered. Slavery was legal. He was not threatening the Union by continuing to act legally and in accordance with the Constitution.

Lincoln turned back to the lectern, grasping the edges with both hands as though to steady it. "We shall try to do our duty. We hope and believe that in no section will a majority so act as to render such extreme measures necessary."

Was Lincoln referring to the threat of secession? Other slave owners talked guardedly about the possibility of seceding, if compromise could not be reached.

Border warfare troubles were also on the speaker's mind. "If I might advise my Republican friends here, I would say to them, 'Leave your Missouri neighbors alone. Have nothing whatever to do with the white people, with slave owners, save in a friendly way.'"

The speech over, Marcus left the hall deeply troubled. On the long, solitary ride the next two days back to his farm, he went over in his mind Lincoln's words, probing for subtleties that might reassure him, an inflection that might permit a more encouraging interpretation of what Lincoln had said.

Could slavery be wrong, even if permitted by law? Marcus felt that people made choices, among them whether to have slaves or not. He chose to have slaves, and he treated them well. If they became sick or died, he lost their productivity. Nothing in his religious beliefs or in his conscience said owning slaves was wrong or immoral.

If this man Lincoln received his new party's nomination, and if Lincoln won the election, unlikely as that appeared, Marcus thought, he might very possibly lose his slaves, and thus the means by which he made his many acres of land productive. The implications of such a great financial loss depressed Marcus, and he felt hugely discouraged. He began to feel that the migration with his family to Missouri was about to become a disaster.

Never before had he considered leaving their new home and going elsewhere, because what he had achieved in Missouri exceeded his expectations. But now he realized that he might lose much of what he had gained. If this happened, Marcus felt he could not begin again.

4

Even in winter, there was work that needed to be done. Slaves cut firewood, broke up the skin of ice that quickly formed in watering troughs for the livestock, and pitched hay from the barn lofts into the horse stalls. They milked the cows, curried the horses, mended wood fences, cleared brush, and built new cabins when additional slaves were bought. With Christmas less than two weeks away, the women cut greenery and brought it into the house to festoon the great hearth, the stair railing, and the door at the front of the house.

Each morning Marchus conferred with Jed about the work to be done that day. Born in Kentucky of Virginia stock, Jed had been foreman on the Gill plantation back in Bath County. Lanky, face like a hound dog with a long, pointed nose, deep-blue patient eyes, ears too large, and scraggly brown hair, Jed was forever taking off his floppy hat, scratching his head as he talked, then easing the hat back on, tugging at the brim so it fit just right. Below his blanched forehead, the face was scarred by weather.

"Been meaning to tell you, Colonel Gill, ol' Jim ain't been doing well lately."

Jim, a slave now well into his seventies, was the field hand who had dutifully kept an eye on Marcus when, as a boy, Marcus rode the mare alone in the pasture. In recent years, Jim helped out in the stable, grooming the horses, carrying water.

"Not well a'tall. He now mostly–" Jed paused, thinking on what he had to say, as was his way. "Just takin' to his bed, seems like." He tugged again at the brim of his hat. "Effie says he ain't eat noth'n but thin soup and a little corn bread." He turned his head to spit tobacco juice, and switched the plug to the other side. "Spect you all might want to know."

Marcus went to Jim's cabin, at the far end of two facing rows of log huts, east of the big hay barn. A stretch of scrabble ground, punctuated by spare clumps of rough, resilient weed, separated the cabin rows. In fair weather, children rolled iron hoops in the dust, made doll figures out of cornhusks, or sometimes sat silent on the stoops, watching. Now the yard was empty.

Marcus tapped softly at the plank door. Effie, the old slave's wife, younger by maybe ten years, opened the door. Her face was smooth-skinned, with high cheekbones, her gray-black hair pulled back from a pensive face. Her eyes worried, Effie motioned her master in. She wore a thin gray shawl, pulled close around the neck, over a colorless cotton dress reaching to her bare feet.

The room, darkened by coarse cloth hung across the windows, was chilly despite the fire in the stove. The air smelled of wood smoke, greens simmering slowly in a pot, and a dank, woodsy odor like the forest after rain. Marcus had not been there before. A table, two chairs pushed under, an old leather trunk, and an iron bed against one wall were the only furnishings. The timbered floor, laid by Jim himself, was scrub-clean, with a lingering smell of linseed oil.

Marcus approached the bed. Jim lay along one side, stretched out on his back, a rough blanket pulled to the collar of his long-johns. Hands clasped loosely on his thin chest, crimped gray hair now gone white. Marcus was startled by the sight of the shrunken body, collarbones protruding harshly, neck long and thin, charcoal skin slack.

He remembered the strong, laughing man he'd known as a child, patiently showing him how to hold the bowed wood handle of the great scythe. Jim had stood behind him, the slave's huge black body enveloping his own, the muscular arms, the large hands alongside his as he struggled to hold the curving blade. Take it firmly in both hands, about this far apart, Jim had showed him, and swing the blade easily, back and forth, smooth-like, with one motion of the body, right to left, right to left, and back again. Their bodies had moved together, the child's body guided by the gentle force around him.

Marcus placed his hand lightly on Jim's shoulder. The eyes opened, focused on Marcus, questioned whom it might be, then knew. A gnarled hand left the security of the hands clasped together, and reached out. Marcus took the outstretched hand in both of his and held it, the hand feverish, the skin dry and rough. All strength was gone from the grasp. A strong emotion suddenly swept through him like a gust of wind across a field of wheat, bending the pliant stalks of grain with its sudden force.

Effie sobbed, raised both hands to her face. She pulled

out one of the chairs and sank down, feet tucked distract-
edly beneath her.

Marcus leaned down and whispered a few words into the
old man's ear, but the slave gave no sign of having heard.
After a moment, the recognition in his eyes faded, then his
hand slowly pulled away to rejoin the other resting on his
chest.

Eyes moist, Marcus again placed his hand lightly on the
old man's shoulder, then turned to go. He looked about the
cabin, stark and gray.

Effie stood up, but kept her eyes directed toward the floor.
Her arms hung by her side, the hands loose.

Marcus remained unmoving, a brooding, puzzled look
on his face. He then gazed at Effie, as if she had unexpectedly entered the room. In a low voice he asked if there was
anything she needed.

Effie raised her head, and looked at him. Marcus saw an
instant flare of anger. Effie's stare confronted him, unyield-
ing. Then the fire vanished, as if suddenly drenched by water. She shook her head, and looked away.

Marcus left the cabin.

The following evening, after supper, when Marcus sat
alone at his desk writing a letter to his son Turner, Mary
Jane came to the door of the room. Jed needed to speak to
him, she said. Marcus stepped outside, where Jed stood sol-
emnly waiting, holding his shapeless hat in both hands.

Jim was dead. Died about suppertime.

Marcus thanked Jed for coming. "I want to bury him in
the family graveyard, here on the farm," Marcus said. "In
the morning, I'll show you just where."

Jed's eyes questioned, but he said nothing. "I've been

thinking about it," Marcus added.

The grave was dug next morning in a plot of ground chosen hurriedly two years ago, when the infant son of Marcus and Mary Jane had not survived a three-day fever. The burial place lay on a rise of ground in a pasture some distance back from the house. The site chosen for the old slave was in a far corner of the cemetery, now enclosed with a waist-high black-iron fence. Marcus and Mary Jane agreed that Effie would someday be laid next to her husband. Back in Kentucky, Negro nursemaids and long-time house servants were sometimes buried in an abbreviated row of graves along the rear of the family cemetery.

A simple burial service was held late in the afternoon. The wind, now abruptly out of the northwest, was keen-edged. Oak leaves, russet red and dull gold, lay packed underfoot, touched with frost. Enormous, cushiony white clouds moved across the sky. Sunlight flooded the ground; then, fleet-footed, hastily fled, leaving the landscape bereft and shadowless.

On the other side of the open grave from Marcus and Mary Jane, the assembled slaves stood motionless, two and three deep around the mound of freshly dug earth. Women dressed in ragged coats, scant cotton dresses, and shawls about their heads, stood quietly next to their men who wore cast-off bulky dark coats and hats that covered their heads when working in the fields. Effie, weeping, waited near the torn edge of the grave, her thin body supported by two of the younger field hands.

Mary Jane, though dressed warmly, shivered slightly, as much from the emotions she felt as from the sharp air. She could see to one side the grave of her infant son, marked by a small stone, his name clearly visible.

Jed and a work overseer stood apart from the gathering. Sharp-bladed shovels, crusted with mud, lay on the ground behind them, unhidden.

Marcus read a few verses from the New Testament. He had never presided at graveside before, at the death of a slave; he had never thought to do so. Now, he felt some discomfort in the role, yet was oddly compelled to carry out the task.

Concluding with the Lord's Prayer, Marcus spoke the words, his voice barely audible. Mary Jane joined him. The others remained silent.

Marcus bent down, took a handful of the dark soil in his hand, crumbled it, and let it drop from his fingers down into the open grave, on top of the coffin, naked yellow wood discordant against the black earth.

Suddenly, Marcus sensed that he was no longer needed, that he should not be there. He looked across at Effie, whose bare hands were clutched at her breast. Her tear-flooded eyes gazed through and past him, as if fixated on an object beyond, beyond his vision. Marcus studied the expressionless, downturned faces of these creatures whose lives he owned. It was as if they were strangers, newly met. The open grave that lay between them was an abyss that grew far beyond its narrow boundaries, a vastness far beyond anything he had felt or known before.

Quietly, Marcus took Mary Jane's arm, and led her away, down the hill, back toward the house.

They had gone almost halfway when, very faint at first, Marcus heard voices, low and rhythmic, the words muffled. The slaves had begun singing, a chant more than a song, uncertain and tentative. The sound was restrained, mournful.

Marcus and Mary Jane stopped, and looked back. It was as if the gathering of individual slaves had fused into one large black shadow against the darkening earth, a strange and new presence. Separate faces became lost, cloaked by the mask of rapidly fading light. At that distance, no lips appeared to move, yet sound emanated from the dark mass, a sad, rich flow of song passed down from generations long ago, from a foreign land.

Engrossed, Marcus and Mary Jane listened. The strangeness of what they witnessed unexpectedly disturbed Marcus. It was like an unidentified sound that awakens one suddenly at night from profound sleep, frightening because the source is not known, can only be imagined.

There arose in his mind the somber figure of Lincoln stepping forward on the narrow platform in Leavenworth, defying those who would keep slavery, summoning those who do to confront the moral issue. But how? Marcus asked. How could I free them? He did not have an answer.

After little more than a long moment, the voices in the distance subsided, then ceased. Without speaking, the slaves turned away from the grave, and walked to their cabins in stillness.

5

Winter nights descended quickly in January, leadening the countryside in isolating blackness. Gathered at the supper table, which was lit by a coal-oil lamp, the family sat with Marcus at one end and his wife at the other. Will Quantrill sat on one side, Leah and her two youngest sisters across from him. Millie had already fed the younger children and put them to bed.

Will talked easily about growing up in Ohio, eldest son of a teacher who later became a school principal. Marcus respected Will's obvious intelligence and was pleased by his occasional lyrical descriptions. As a Southerner, Marcus enjoyed telling and listening to stories. They brightened the bleak winter evenings like a fire warming the room.

"My father died five years ago, when I was seventeen," Will said. "I decided to get out on my own. So I went to Indiana, learned some Latin and surveying. Then I crossed over to Illinois. Taught school there awhile. Felt good about that."

Leah watched Will as he talked. His soft, persuasive voice drew her into his narration. Will's upper eyelids drooped in such a way that he looked vaguely foreign, even slightly mysterious. His voice was without the Southern inflections of her own family and many of their neighbors, and that made him seem even more different to her. He often looked directly at her while he spoke, holding her eyes as if he were talking only to her, rather than relating incidents of his life to all those around the table. Marcus noted Leah's fascination with their guest, and Will's obvious playing to the young woman. He and Mary Jane exchanged glances tinged with concern.

"Colonel Gill," Will said after a time, courteously turning the conversation away from himself, "I suppose life here in Missouri is considerably different from what it was back in Kentucky. Missouri is as far South as I've ever been, so I can't really imagine what it must have been like where you came from. Did people leave you alone, let you live the way you wanted to live?"

Marcus, his fork pausing in mid-air, looked thoughtfully at Will. "Yes, I believe that's true," he said. "I never thought of it quite that way, but I think it's true." He resumed eating. "We'd been there a long time, you understand. My family goes back to the Revolution, maybe farther. My father's grandfather fought in the war, that I know. He was a captain of cavalry. My father still has a big farm, back in Kentucky. You ask if we had more freedom. Well, I—"

"I meant, was it easier for you to do whatever you wanted to do? Without other folks interfering. Not letting you accomplish what you set out to do. I mean, no one thought anything about your owning slaves, I'd guess. And of course, there weren't no Kansans riling things up like they're doing around here now."

"Yes, I expect we did have more freedom, if you put it that way," Marcus said again. "I think the difference is that the way my family lived, we'd been living that way for quite a few generations. Families like ours from Kentucky, or from Virginia, often go back a hundred years in the South, sometimes longer. But here in Jackson County, and I'd guess other counties in the western part of the state, settlers haven't been there anywhere near that long. And besides—"

"Of course not, Papa," Leah broke in. "After all, Missouri became a state less than forty years ago."

"That's right," Marcus said. "Virginia, for example, was first a colony, then a state. It's been a state seventy years, now. Kentucky almost as long. That's maybe two generations before Missouri obtained statehood. So our way of life in the South was established a long time ago. We've had slavery more than two hundred years. It's part of our life, always was. There's some folks here in Missouri, and certainly west of us, don't understand that."

Leah again spoke up. "You said you felt more free in Kentucky, Papa. I don't understand that. Except for those horrible raiders, I've never thought I was any less free than I was back home. And I was eleven when we came west." She thought a moment. "That's pretty old."

Marcus smiled. "Sometimes it's the differences you feel, more than the differences you can see," he said. "Back home, we generally kept to ourselves. I'd help my neighbors out, if they needed it, and they'd do the same. But not being dependent on others was a part of being free. If you become obligated to someone, then that person can begin to gain control over you, to expect things. Someday there'll come a time when they tell you what to do, contrary to what you want. That's already what's happening with our federal government."

"I'd feel the same way," Will said. "I couldn't sit still for someone else deciding what I should do."

Marcus nodded. "As I said, owning slaves was accepted. Nobody thought much about it. But it's not the same here, even though I'm told that there are large numbers of slaves in Missouri. Many of them are in counties east of here, south of the Missouri River. But some folks can't seem to accept slavery."

Marcus, having finished eating, moved his chair back a little from the table. "Most of the families in Missouri who didn't come from the South, came from the East, from New England. They didn't know much about slavery, because slavery was not common there. I've come to believe they resent anyone who owns slaves."

Mary Jane nodded in agreement.

"Others have religious attitudes against slavery," Marcus continued, "but scripture doesn't condemn slavery. Fact is, there were many slaves in times of the Bible. Paul wrote the book of Philemon, for example, as a letter to be sent with Onesimus, an escaped slave, that Paul was sending back to his master, Philemon. If Paul had looked on slavery as something bad or evil, he would have spoken out. Later, Paul even says, 'Slaves, be obedient to your masters.'"

"And the disciple Peter," Mary Jane added. "Peter said: 'Slaves, accept the authority of your masters with all deference, not only those who are kind and gentle, but also those who are harsh.'"

"So the Bible accepts slavery," Marcus said. "I wouldn't

mind folks objecting to my owning slaves, if they'd just keep it to themselves. But they don't. It's as if they just can't keep from speaking out, letting you know they're against it. And they make you feel like you were doing something morally wrong, when it isn't wrong."

"Colonel Gill was respected back in Kentucky," Mary Jane said. "He'll think I shouldn't say so, because it doesn't sound modest, but he was. Besides, we've always treated our slaves right. And he was known for being a leader in the state militia. And farmers we knew often asked his advice. The sawmill he owned was a fine one. They built their houses and barns with the lumber the mill turned out."

"Well, times are changing," Marcus said. "I know that. I just wish I had some say as to what's happening."

Supper over, the two men went into the parlor. Marcus offered Will a cigar, lit it, then put the flame to his own. "Just last week, I stopped in the bank at Westport to ask about a loan to buy yearlings. I was told to talk to a bank officer I'd never seen before. Said his name was Schilling, that he'd just come over from St. Louis. He said the bank was investing money for eastern investors. I'd think there's enough money in the banks right here, without bringing in that eastern money. Besides, what do they know about farming out west, out in Missouri?"

Marcus drew on his cigar, the smoke hovering around him. "St. Louis is also full of Germans, I hear. I don't know what draws them from back east. Republicans are registering Germans to vote as fast as they can sign them up, to do away with slavery." His tone showed disgust. "What right have they to do that?"

Marcus got up from his chair and stood next to the fire, flicking a long ash from his cigar into the coals. "That banker from St. Louis knew I farmed with slaves, and I could tell he was uneasy talking with me. He'd look at some papers on his desk, or off behind me, as if he was expecting another customer to appear any moment. Fact of the matter is, when he asked me where my farm was located, he didn't know where New Santa Fe is, and he had no idea how long I've been in Jackson County. Thought I'd just come west."

"What did you do?" Will asked. "When he treated you that way."

"What could I do? It might have been a strain, if I hadn't taken out the loan, although maybe I'd have gotten by without it. But I've always gotten a loan before, to buy yearlings, so I thought I might just as well do it this year, too. Bankers like things to be as they've been before. And I think they like my business, although they don't often let you know that."

"I'd have walked out of the bank if they'd treated me that way," Will said. "And I'd have looked for a chance to get even." His face flushed. "Could you have gone to another bank? Gone someplace else?"

"Yes, I suppose I could have. There are other banks farther north, in the City of Kansas, near the river. Maybe next time I will."

Marcus sat down again, stretching out his legs, and gazed into the fire. "I think what the bankers and the black Republicans are after is to force land owners like me to break up our farms. They want to put us in a position where we have to sell off parcels to small farmers who would own sixty, maybe eighty acres. That way, they can do most of the work themselves, without slaves, and without hiring labor." He looked thoughtful as he drew on his cigar. "But I know that a man can't make much money farming that way. All he can do is struggle to make enough to provide the necessities for his family."

"What would you do, Colonel Gill," Will asked, "if that came to pass? If you had to break up your property?"

Gill took a moment before continuing. "Well, if they take my slaves away from me, that's what I'd be forced to do. I don't see any other way. I'd lose all that money I've already invested in slaves, and I'd have no way of working the farm. Hiring field hands is a lot more costly and undependable than working your own slaves."

Abruptly, Marcus stood up. "But I don't want to break up my farm. The law says I can own slaves. The law says they're my property. The law says I can get them back, if they try to run away. Besides, it took me a lot of years, a big invest-ment, to build up this place. I'm not going to let anyone walk in and take it away."

Sparks leaped upward as Marcus tossed another log on top of the radiant embers. "I'd hate to give in, because I think those Northerners just want for themselves what I've already got." Then, as if to himself, he added, "What hurts the most is they don't have any respect for us. They just don't think we're as good as them." He tossed the cigar butt into the flames. "And I don't like that. I just can't accept that."

6

At the schoolhouse near Stanton, Will sat at his desk, writing his mother in Ohio. The silence was punctuated only by the popping of the iron stove as the surface began to cool from the dying fire.

When you write let me know all that you have time to write about, for I feel anxious to know something about home and the village of my boyhood more than I have heretofore and I cannot really say why it is so, but I think of it more, and have lately visited it in my dreams, which was quite rare before, it may be because my mind has become more settled, and my mind must be employed in some way, and I suppose that is the most natural. I wish to know all that has happened of note lately, and I would like to be there and think I will be (if I live) in the course of the summer. . . .

As Will wrote, nostalgia for his boyhood engulfed him. At the same time, impatience and anger welled up, forcing aside the poignant memories of his youth. Restlessness

47

gnawed at his fragile sense of well being. He felt as if events were careening past him, causing his present life to collapse under the guise of its hapless, commonplace events.

On the journey to Utah and Colorado with the Russell-Majors freight wagons, he had confronted the hardships of winter, meager supplies of wild game, and sometimes churlish companions, but had remained in command of himself.

Will now ached for recognition beyond that of a schoolteacher. He saw himself as a leader of men. He prided himself on his skill with firearms, his adroitness on horseback. He knew that, unlike some men, he was able to remain levelheaded when in danger, and to think clearly and boldly.

But now, seated at the schoolhouse desk, Will felt trapped, shunted from his true calling, however unknown. He realized that he had to find a way to break out, to become engaged in a larger destiny. He felt as if events taking place about him were like a rushing, plunging stream, but he was only a bystander, fixed helplessly on the bank while the current moved swiftly and surely to a place he wished to be. Unless he could wade into that stream and be carried by it to whatever lay before him, he would never find his place in history. The more he considered his present circumstance, the more determined he became to leap from the river's bank into the torrent of water.

One Sunday in early spring after the noon meal, Leah and Will rode out along the wide swath marking the barrier between Missouri and the Kansas Territory, the trail used by wagons hauled by ox teams in the Santa Fe trade. Although her mother was watchful of Leah's relationship with Will, they often rode together, talking and laughing, even sometimes disagreeing on political issues. Leah was drawn to Will's untroubled self-confidence, his enthusiasm, but she did not grasp the extent to which he grappled with frustrated ambition. She correctly perceived the deep, unaccountable undercurrents in his nature, often concealed by his eager manner, his appetite for new exploits, yet she found these forces strangely exciting, inexplicably appealing.

His restlessness and dissatisfaction with his life disturbed her, however, because she saw that they threatened their relationship. She feared that he would soon leave her family, leave her. She also sensed from the little Will confided to her that he yearned mightily to be admired, that he sought above all else a role that would bring him prominence. With a woman's mysterious premonition, Leah envisioned Will thrust up above the crowd, lifted high on the shoulders of other men. Perhaps that accounted in part for the strong attraction he had for her.

Will was older than Leah by six years. He thought her very beautiful, possessing spirited courage, an audacious mind of her own. The fact that he ascribed these same characteristics to himself had not occurred to him. When she talked with fervor about the issues of slavery and states rights, he listened, but did not consider that as a woman she could ever act upon such beliefs. To him, action in conflict was the only course.

Through a gate they entered a pasture far removed from the house. Wild coneflowers, pale purple with yellow centers, were splashed across the dark green fields like flower petals on a full-flowing skirt. Stretching to the western horizon, the sweeping grasslands of the Kansas Territory seemed vast, unending. From the direction of Independence, a wagon train, barely visible at that distance, westward-bound for Santa Fe, moved imperceptibly toward them, brown dust suspended motionless in the air above. Teams of oxen, dark heads lowered, great shoulders working in the yokes melded with the ground. Teamsters walking beside the animals resembled stick figures, wielding their long whips languorously, as if imagined in a dream.

Will spurred his mare, colored a deep chestnut, across the open pasture. Leah followed, urging the thoroughbred into a graceful canter along the shadowed edge of the timber. A gift from her father for her sixteenth birthday, the horse had white socks on its forelegs, and flaxen mane and tail that drifted fluidly in the wind.

Then Leah took the lead, and together they raced, the warm, scented breeze rushing past them. Exhilarated, Will whooped and hollered, holding onto his hat with one hand.

Leah leaned into the wind, and bent close to the mare's mane, urging her horse forward. Not breaking the canter, she began to edge ahead of Will. The hooves of the horses drummed a muffled pattern on the taut skin of the earth. Will held his horse in check, letting Leah pull away, and watched her dark hair streaming out behind. Her lithe figure, moving in rhythm, fused gracefully with that of the mount beneath her.

At the far reach of the pasture, the timber turned to the south, following the creek. As they approached the timber, Leah reined in, brought her horse to a halt, and slid out of the saddle, her face flushed with excitement. Laughing softly, Will rode up behind, kicked his boots free from the stirrups, threw one leg over the saddle, and eased himself off the horse. Taking both sets of reins, he led the horses to a tree and looped the reins around a greening branch. Together, arms around each other's waists, they strolled deeper into the woods.

Leah chatted amiably, Will listened. He relished the slight swaying of her body, the swishing of her long skirt as they walked leisurely through the still winter-thin timber to the creek's bank. Blackbirds, scolding noisily, fluttered anxiously from one branch to another at the top of the trees. Along the creek, redbuds threw out splashes of lavender against gray branches.

They stopped near the trunk of a great oak. Leah turned toward Will. He brought her close against him and kissed her, then kissed her again. Leah's arms reached up about his neck, one hand lightly caressing the back of his neck, the other hand drawing him even closer. She kissed him earnestly, while with one hand he explored the familiar curve of her hip, the delicate indentation where her back melded into the fullness below. Without speaking, they sank down onto the cool, thick grass, hidden by the trees and concealing undergrowth.

Sunlight reaching through branches overhead, like trellises in a garden, patterned the ground with splashes of fresh color. A warm current of air finding its way along the sun-drenched, sky-reaching space above the creek channel stirred blades of grass and rustled dry leaves on the ground, yet otherwise passed unnoticed.

Leah sat on a large log, combing her hair with her fingers, then smoothed the wool skirt about her legs, removing bits of leaves and grass. Will sat down next to her, watching the capable movement of her hands, the graceful way she preened herself. Smiling, she grasped his hand and brought it to her lips, kissing it.

Then, her face becoming serious, Leah asked the question that had been on her mind the last few days. "Will, what are you going to do when you finish teaching school? You've only got two more weeks."

Will gazed off into the timber before replying. "I've been thinking about it. You know I want to get into where things are happening," he said. "I just can't stay out of it. I just can't sit by the side of the road, watching. So I've been thinking about joining up with a gang of bushwhackers holed up west of Independence. They've already had some skirmishes with raiders, and gone over into the Territory once or twice themselves, to get back at those devils. I hear they've done well for themselves."

Leah nodded. Her father had said he felt good about the skill and bold attacks of the bushwhackers. He thought they were forcing the Kansas guerrillas to think twice about crossing over to harass and steal from farmers in the county. "But they're just boys, aren't they, Will? Just farm boys? What do they know about fighting?"

"They do real good, all things considered. Farm boys know how to shoot, how to live off the land, and they like a little excitement. Besides, they're tough. All they need is a good leader, someone who's got experience. And a place in the bush to hide out, away from roads, and something to eat when they get hungry."

Will looked around, as if appraising whether this stand of timber might be such a place. "That's what's good about summer. Plenty of cover and wild game. Besides that, lots of folks appreciate what they do, and give them food and supplies, even ammunition and guns. If war comes, there's several good gangs I'd join up with. Heck, I don't think I need to wait 'til there's a war. I could do it right now."

Leah frowned. "But why not, Will? Why not wait? Papa needs you, and there's plenty else you can do."

"But that's just it, Leah, I don't want to be doing anything else. I'm real good with guns, and I don't get scared when there's fighting, and I think I could soon have my own gang, with me as the leader. That's what I'd really like to do. I want to lead a gang."

"You could fight for the South, Will, if there's war. That's what Turner said he would do. And my brother Enoch, teaching school down in Texas. He wrote home that he's ready to enlist in the army of the South, if fighting begins."

Picking up a stick from the ground, Will took out a sheath knife, and began skinning off the bark.

"I don't think as how I'd like being in the regular army, Leah, taking orders from someone else. If they'd make me a captain, in the cavalry, then maybe I would, but even then, I'd be taking orders from someone higher up, and that's not what I want. Anyway, can you imagine me saluting some officer who's maybe just learned to ride a horse and shoot a gun, and I'm suppose to do whatever he says?"

Leah smiled, and gave Will a playful shove, before becoming serious again. "Papa thinks the whole country will be at war, if Lincoln gets elected by people who don't like slavery. He thinks it's up to Lincoln to find a way for us Southerners to keep our slaves, at least the slaves we already own. He just doesn't see how any president could take away the property we already own, and not compensate us for it."

Will laid the knife and stick on the log, and eased the pistol holster at his waist a little to one side, to relieve the pressure against his hip. "You'd think slave owners weren't rightful citizens, Leah, entitled to their property, to protection, like everyone else." He sharpened the end of the stick into a two-sided point. "If it comes to war, the colonel figures bushwhackers can keep Union troops off balance by taking them by surprise, killing and wounding enough of them to do some damage, then getting away as fast as they can ride, and hiding out for a time. I think he's right."

Leah gently touched Will's arm. "Well, you've got to do what you think you should. There's no doubt you're a good rider, Will, and I've seen you shoot, you're the best there is." She looked around, taking in the burgeoning beauty of the timber. Unseen, a woodpecker hammered away at a dead tree, a solitary staccato. "Well, guess we'd best be going," she said regretfully. "Papa will be wondering why we're not back."

Will put his arm around Leah's shoulders. Walking slowly back to where the tethered horses stood waiting, they pressed close, shoulders and thighs firmly against each other. Leah reached out to stroke the white blaze on her mare's face. The horse nuzzled Leah's shoulder, searching for a carrot tucked in a pocket of her dress.

"I feel I've got something important to do, Leah, and I need to get on with it. Situation's getting more and more serious all the time." Will untied the mare's bridle from the tree branch. "Neighbors who don't own slaves, they think their neighbors who do are just no good. Those who own slaves, they're never sure which neighbor might be giving information to the raiders, helping them out when they come stealing livestock and burning barns. A person can't never know for sure which side another person else might be on. Folks hide what they think, so you can't tell." His voice rose slightly. "But you got to stand up to them, when they turn against you. You just got to do that. A man's got no other choice. Leastwise, not one he can live with."

Leah looked at Will, saw the hard look in his eyes, the

tautness at the corners of his mouth. "I love you, Will. I worry about you, and I don't want you to get killed."

Riding back to the house, they did not again talk about the possibility of war, or about when Will might leave.

7

One morning in early May, Marcus and Jed went looking for a stray calf. Will had left the day before to ride over to Independence to tend to business of his own, planning to be back the next day. Marcus rode his dapple-gray gelding, a fine thoroughbred with great endurance and a strong gait.

"Jed, let's search the timber this side of the creek. You start up toward the north, I'll go down to the far end. We'll work back to the middle." Jed nodded his head. "Fire your pistol if you find the calf. I'll do the same." Marcus gestured toward the .58 caliber single-shot rifle slung across his back.

In good spirits, Marcus cantered off, feeling the energy of a new planting season flow through his body. Insects droned in the air and tall grass. The sky was spring-water clear, the breeze filled with the rich scent of white-flowered clover. Rugged split-rail fences, cut from timber on his farm, sundered with an ax and skillfully interlocked, enclosed the pastures where cows with spirited calves browsed the green fields.

Marcus looked across those fields. A white, translucent haze, lying gossamer-like in the folds of the valley, softened the shape of his house, his barns, the clusters of other farm buildings which stood solidly on the flank of the hill. Faint voices far off, like the buzz of bees drifting in the sun from one flower to the next, touched him with their familiar sound. Marcus felt deeply satisfied with what he saw: his land, transformed into richly productive soil, the product of his vision, his ability, and the leavening of his capital.

He reined in the gelding, and left the pasture, entering the shadows of the timber. Methodically, Marcus worked through the wooded area lying west of the creek, searching for the calf. He stopped frequently, listening for sounds of the young animal thrashing through the underbrush. He heard only the wind stirring the trees, the raucous cries of crows, and the gelding's snorting as he lifted his legs free of the brush.

Marcus decided to ride to the creek so his horse could drink. They passed through a natural clearing, free of brush, and abruptly came to the bank. Creek water, muddy from the spring rains, as deep as the underside of a horse's belly, moved sluggishly.

Five horsemen sat motionless on the other side, no more than sixty feet away, watching him. The men were young, all bearded. They were not in uniform, but were similarly dressed. They wore hats pulled low on their heads, darkening their faces, and were heavily armed. Marcus recognized the .44 caliber Colt carbines two of the men held, stock butts resting on their thighs as they watched him; these men were not farmers, nor were they soldiers. The other horsemen carried rifles on slings across their chest and pistols shoved into wide leather belts at the waist.

No one spoke. Marcus knew they didn't belong on his land. If he turned and ran, they'd shoot him in the back.

"You own this land?" called out the leader, erect in the saddle, scorn in his voice.

"I do."

"What might your name be?"

"Marcus Gill."

Two of the riders looked at their leader, then back at Marcus. Their right hands rested on the handles of pistols in holsters at their side.

Marcus took the initiative. "What brings you here?"

"We've got business in the area."

Marcus paused, his voice offhand. "Where'd you boys come from?"

"West of here." That would be Kansas Territory.

One of the men leaned closer to the leader and said something. The leader nodded, and shouted across to Marcus, "I want you to ease that rifle off your back and toss it onto the ground."

Marcus looked back, without moving. He listened for sounds of Jed, but heard none. "This is my property. I don't intend to do that. You boys are trespassing. Why don't you just head on back home."

The second man again spoke under his breath to the leader and then yanked his gun from the holster.

Impatient, the leader called out, "You best do what I say, rebel. We're planning on taking your horse and whatever money you got back at the house, and–"

A rifle shot exploded out of the timber off to one side of the men. The leader's body snapped forward, shot through the chest. His arms hung useless on either side of the horse's neck. The horse shied to one side and the body tumbled to the ground.

The remaining horsemen turned quickly, shouting in confusion, firing their pistols in the direction of the sound, but a second shot struck another man in the back, knocking him out of the saddle. One boot caught in the stirrup, and the man's limp body fell to one side of his mount, dragging on the ground, but was torn loose by the heavy underbrush as the frightened horse bolted through the timber.

Will Quantrill stepped from behind a tree, firing rapidly, a pistol in each hand. Marcus had his rifle at his shoulder in an instant, the .58 caliber sounding like a canon among the trees. The crashing ball of lead swept a third man off his horse as he attempted to flee. The two remaining gunmen, firing frantically, wheeled their horses, but bullets from Will's guns struck the fourth man who slid sideways from his saddle and plunged to the ground. By then the one remaining guerrilla had vanished into the timber.

Gunpowder smoke, cobalt blue and acrid, drifted in the still air, carved into rectangular shafts by sunlight filtering through the trees.

Marcus rapidly reloaded, then rode the gelding through the creek and up the bank. He dismounted, holding his rifle muzzle up in one hand.

Thrusting the Colt revolvers back into their holsters, Will picked up the rifled musket he had dropped to the ground after killing the gang's leader, reloaded it with a single linen cartridge and primer, and leaned the gun against a nearby tree. He walked up to the riderless horses, soothing each of them with soft-spoken words, stroking their necks, then tied the reins to a tree.

The body of the guerrilla band's leader lay face up on the ground, eyes astonished, arms outstretched above the head. Will looked at the face. "Jayhawker," he said, and turned the body over with his boot. The other bodies he left alone, uninterested in who they might be.

"I seen them going into th' other side of the timber when I was coming back from Independence," Will said. "Figured they might be up to no good, that they weren't one of us."

Marcus nodded, and said matter-of-factly, "Glad you came along. Thanks, Will."

Will shrugged. "That's what I'm here for, ain't it?" and grinned.

Marcus later sent some field hands to bury the dead raiders in the timber, instructing that brush and dead leaves be placed over the upturned earth to hide them.

8

When school ended in the early spring of 1860, Will was anxious to move on. He said good-bye to the colonel and his family, and rode off into Kansas Territory, heading for Lawrence, fifty miles to the west. Marcus wondered why Will would go there. Like many Missouri slave owners, Marcus detested Lawrence. Its leadership dominated by abolitionist New Englanders, Lawrence was the spawning ground of much of the guerrilla activity harassing Missouri farmers. But Will said he had unfinished business in Lawrence, that he had scores to settle.

Later in the summer, Henry Chiles told Marcus that Will had been arrested by the sheriff in Douglas County, where Lawrence was the county seat, for burglary, larceny, and arson. While charges were pending, however, he slipped away and disappeared. Marcus was skeptical of the arrest, knowing that Lawrence was rife with opposing factions.

When he told Leah, she scoffed at the charges, but looked worried.

By autumn, under Jed's watchful eye, the slaves had harvested the summer's crops. Once again they filled the cribs with corncobs shucked of husks, the kernels dull yellow and brittle-hard. They scythed the wheat, loading the sheaths into mule-drawn wagons, then lifted forkfuls of the hay up into the barn lofts for winter feed for the livestock. Other slaves butchered cows, hogs, and sheep, smoking the meat or salting it down to cure, and hung hams, all for the approaching winter.

Mary Jane, pregnant and weary from the months of carrying her seventh child, hoped the baby would come soon. She was thirty-eight years old. The loss of their son born the first year after they arrived in Missouri was still a poignant, aching memory, yet she did not confide to Marcus that having another baby worried her, that she didn't know whether she could mother yet another child.

Moving about slowly, Mary Jane oversaw the women slaves who boiled fresh vegetables from the acre-wide garden for canning, or made fruit preserves and jellies, and shelled sweet corn, preserving it in salt brine. They scoured the underground fruit cellar and replenished the earthy smelling woodbins with sweet potatoes, carrots, apples, plums, and other fruit. Laid down in beds of straw, the food would last in the cool darkness.

Events of each day on the farm proceeded with accustomed rhythm, yet violence remained a dark stain on the countryside. Marcus learned that attacks by abolitionists were more frequent, bolder, and more virulent, despite increasing counteraction by Missouri bushwhackers. To his dismay, he found that anti-slavery attitudes smoldered beneath everyday relationships with townspeople, such as at the marketplace on visits into Westport. With slight provocation, resentments burst into angry recriminations, often when least expected.

Unlike states farther south, Missouri had persistent ties to the Union, especially in St. Louis, on the eastern edge of the state. Commerce and industry in that city on the Mississippi River fixed its eyes on New England's advanced prosperity, on New England's proficiency and mounds of capital. Marcus knew this, and he chafed under the knowledge, because he felt powerless to counter these eastern influences.

There was no word from Will. Leah thought of him often, longed for the unrevealed relationship they had shared, but she received no letters, nor was any message passed along from him. Meanwhile, Jesse Noland, son of a prominent family near Independence, was courting her. Marcus and Mary Jane knew the Nolands, Southerners like themselves, and favored the match, if that were the outcome. They had hoped she would not fall in love with Will; he was too unsettled, too unpredictable.

The first Sunday in November 1860, the winds were raw, the ground frozen, skies unchanging in slate-gray overcast. The country continued to struggle with the issue of slavery. Now it might find resolution. Within days, a national election was to be held to choose the next president of the United States.

There were four candidates, Lincoln among them, heading the Republican party, formed only six years ago. Marcus strongly favored John Breckinridge, who was forthright in his defense and support of slavery. Stephen Douglas from Illinois, a candidate who also had support in the South, was more compromising in his views toward slavery. Marcus felt that by being conciliatory, Douglas weakened the pro-slavery position.

John Bell was the fourth candidate. He ran on the Union Party platform that offered concessions to both abolitionists and those favoring the expansion of slavery. Again, Marcus believed that slavery could only be weakened by failure to take a non-compromising position on the issue.

Hearing Lincoln speak in Leavenworth and having thought frequently about what he had said, Marcus conceded that Lincoln was a convincing candidate. He may have appeared awkward, and his voice high-pitched, even disagreeable when he spoke too forcefully, but the man seemed truthful, well meaning, and resolute. As difficult as it was to accept the view, Marcus had come to believe that Lincoln might win the election; and that if he did, he would do all he could as president to carry through on his resolve to end slavery.

Therefore, Marcus determined that he would raise the question after church in New Santa Fe, when some of the men stayed to talk. Every vote in the country was important.

There were about a dozen or more that stayed behind. In the preacher's study, they pulled up straight-back wood chairs and a couple of benches, close to the round-bellied iron stove. Despite the cold outside, the room was too warm, the air close.

Not all those present might agree, Marcus realized, that Breckinridge was the man to vote for, but he felt that if anyone wavered on which candidate to choose, he would persuade him to cast a ballot for Breckinridge.

"You know about the election next week," Marcus began. Several heads nodded. "Other candidates are up for election, not just who's going to be president. Those positions are for the Congress and our state legislature in Jefferson City. But who's going to lead the country, that's the most important decision."

Marcus looked around at other faces in the room. They were mostly farmers like him, all slave owners except the preacher, who he knew was personally opposed to slavery, and a lawyer, whose opinion he didn't know. The same was true for several others present; while they didn't own slaves, neither had they made known whether or not they were against slavery.

"Those running on the Republican ballot," Marcus continued in a level voice, "they're against slavery. That's the party Lincoln belongs to. And that includes Republican candidates for the state legislature and for Congress. The party hasn't been around nearly as long as the Democrats. They think slavery ought to be abolished. They want to set slaves free. Just like I've told some of you I heard Lincoln talking, up in Leavenworth, when he was running for the nomination."

"That'll ruin the country," a man across from Marcus grumbled. "Where do they think all those slaves are going to go? Who's going to feed them, look after them? Where would they live?"

"They're suppose to find jobs, I hear," a farmer said. "But I read in one of the St. Louis newspapers that there might be as many as four million slaves in the country. That doesn't include another half a million Negroes already free, mostly up north or back east."

"I've heard the same thing," Marcus said. "If the slaves are freed, I just can't figure out what they'll do. I wouldn't want to hire my own slaves to work for me in the fields. So where would they go?"

Another man spoke up. "But that's not the only problem. There's a lot of those people up north and back east, white like us, who can't accept the way we live. My wife's family are up in Chicago. They think that because I own slaves, I'm just trash compared with them. They think nothing about meddling, always letting my wife feel like I'm beneath them." His voice rose, and his face showed his agitation. "What I can't tolerate is their preaching to us, saying we're going against God, because we have slaves. It shouldn't concern them. I don't preach back to them about the fact that their family owns a packinghouse. I'm told that men in packing-houses work twelve-hour days under terrible conditions. Children, too. Who are they to take after me?"

"You're right," an older farmer added. "I come from Massachusetts, and the way they treat Irish immigrants in Boston City back there is hard to believe. Irish aren't even considered citizens, and they work for next to nothing in wages. How can they give me a sermon about owning slaves?"

The preacher, who had sat quietly, said "But slavery, owning another human being as if he was nothing more than a work animal, that's just wrong. It isn't right. Doesn't that have to change?"

A newcomer who owned a mill east of town, on the Blue River, spoke up. "I understand your thinking that, Reverend, but Negroes are just not the same as you and me. I've got just the three slaves I use in my mill, and one in my house, but they're only good for what they're doing for me now. I can't imagine how they'd get along otherwise, if I didn't own them, or if somebody like me wasn't looking after them all the time."

Henry Chiles spat into the coal bucket. "Heck, I've got

cousins in South Carolina. Lots of those folks just ain't going to go along with freeing the slaves. My cousins won't. They'll pull out of the Union, if need be." No one was surprised. "Lincoln's so all-fired determined to free the Negroes, maybe he ought to send them off to that place called Liberia, like he once said he'd consider, so they'd have their own way of life. But no one's said he'd pay us for them."

Jesse Johnson, an older farmer whom Marcus greatly respected, shook his head. "Secession ain't the answer. If there's a war, we'll get hurt bad." He tugged on his beard. "Besides, I come here from Illinois because land back home had gotten too costly. But I seen the railroads bring some good, back in Illinois. Those tracks they're laying now, on west from Jefferson City, a war would end that. Bring it to a halt. Railroad companies have already threatened to move the roadbed north, into Nebraska, if there's trouble in Missouri and Kansas. The railroads mean markets we're going to need some day. We'll be left out if we don't have them, both railroads and markets."

Marcus thought of the new banker from St. Louis he'd talked to, and the man's poorly concealed disdain because Marcus owned slaves. He shook his head. "Running a railroad through Missouri also means more people moving here from the east. They'll be going on into Kansas, too, settling there, proving up claims for land from the government."

"And that means Kansas will be free-state," Henry Chiles injected, "because those Easterners will see to it that it happens. They'll vote to prohibit slavery. We'll be up against more folks who don't like what we do. What's more, my slaves will know there's people agitating to set them free."

"What does your father think about this?" Marcus asked Henry. "And how's he getting along? I'm sorry to hear he's been sick."

"We've been worried, no doubt about that, because he seems to be losing his strength, but I'll tell him you asked after him," Henry replied. "Well, I don't agree with him, but he says we might just as well get used to the direction affairs are headed. Thinks we'd do better going along with the Republicans, even giving up slavery, if we have to." Everyone was silent. Henry's father was wealthy and influential in the county. "He says we ought to look at St. Louis, see what a growing economy has done for them. And being on the Mississippi gives them markets as far south as New Orleans. Lots more people with money back in St. Louis, my father says, compared with folks around here. He thinks we can do what they do."

"I just can't accept that, Henry," Marcus said. "Start thinking like a Republican, that is. I've always been a Democrat, and my father before me. Besides, I can't vote for Lincoln when I know he'll take my slaves. What would I do? I'd have to sell most of my land. You know that. Sell it at whatever price I could get, buyers knowing that slavery isn't allowed anymore. The only prospects to buy land would be folks looking for a small place, sixty, maybe eighty acres. And most of those don't have enough money."

Henry shrugged, as if only stating a view other than his own. "Father thinks that's what's coming. People will be moving west to find opportunities they no longer have in the east, where it's mighty crowded. They'll be looking for land to raise a family on. Enough land to support themselves, and lay a little money aside. That's what's already attracting them to settle out in the Territory, where they can homestead, get land for free from the government."

Marcus said nothing. He looked around at other faces,

some as serious as his own. "Well, maybe. Time will tell. But you got to look at it this way, too. The money I've got tied up in slaves is almost half the amount I've got invested in land. How can Lincoln expect me to just throw that away, if he's elected and frees the slaves? Would that be fair?"

"I agree with you, Marcus," Henry said. "I'm just saying what my father thinks." Others nodded their head. Most of the farmers there faced the same financial loss if the right to own slaves was outlawed.

"Marcus," Carter Johnson said, "something else I've been thinking about. You're a Kentucky man, like me. You have two sons, like I do, old enough to fight. What are you going to do if it comes to that?" The Johnson farm was east of town. His oldest son was about Turner's age.

Marcus leaned back on two legs of his chair, and spoke with deep feeling. "Took me more than six years to build up what I have now. I have a baby boy, named after me, buried on the place." The words formed slowly. "Nowadays, going to bed at night, I put a gun on the table and a loaded rifle under the bed. Two of my field hands stay the night in the barn loft, where they can watch the roads to the house, taking turns keeping awake. I put a dinner bell on top of the barn, so they can ring it good and loud, if someone shows up who has no business on my property."

Abruptly, he sat forward, the two front legs of the chair striking the wood floor loud enough to splinter. "I don't want anybody troubling me. I like things the way they are. I'd be willing to stay with the Union, but not if they're going to steal what's mine." Marcus stood up, reaching for his coat and hat. "Lincoln should see that. He should understand that." He shook his head. "I don't know why he doesn't."

A few days after the election, Marcus learned the details

about the results. Jed brought back from Westport a St. Louis newspaper. The Republican Party, whose major plank was the elimination of slavery, had won by a large margin. In those states not seceding, the Republicans got forty-nine percent of the popular vote and a large electoral college majority. However, including all the states, Lincoln and his party received less than forty percent of the popular vote, the remainder divided among the three other candidates. Joyous crowds had taken to the streets in St. Louis, celebrating the victory over slavery. The same was true in big cities back east.

The worst news, unexpected by Marcus, stunned him with all its implications. Missouri chose a delegation whose members would vote eighty-nine to one against secession. Missouri would side with the northern states. As a slave owner, he felt that his own government had expelled him, was forcing him to leave his home and all that he had built.

9

In late November, Mary Jane gave birth to a daughter. They named her Louella, a family name on the Gill side. The baby was healthy, and Marcus was grateful. Yet the assaults on slavery, the lurking danger of another raid, the uncertainty of who was a friend and who was not, suffused his mind to the extent that, by the end of some days, he wondered whether he had the strength to maintain a sense of order in his life.

Less than two weeks later, Will set out from Lawrence with five other men. He had cunningly selected those who rode with him, although they didn't know it, and he didn't tell them why. They had met him only recently and knew him as Charley Hart, an alias he had adopted in the Kansas Territory. They understood he had a reputation as a fierce gunfighter, but found him likable, opposed to slavery, and very confident. Two of the men were Quakers, zealous abolitionists who saw freeing slaves as a religious mission. The others had no firm views on slavery, but sought excitement and the loot they could garner on a raid into Missouri. So, they had accepted Will's proposition that they make a raid into Jackson County to free some slaves and bring back horses to sell in the Lawrence auction.

Will had told them he knew of a wealthy farmer in Jackson County, east of Westport, who owned almost two thousand acres of land, more than twenty slaves, and about a hundred head of horses and mules. The farmer's name was Morgan Walker. He'd make a fine target for a raid, Will said, especially because the farm was located in a remote section of the county.

The men left the outskirts of Lawrence in late afternoon under a heavy, foreboding sky, and rode eastward, toward the Missouri line. Fording the Wakarusa River a few hours later, their horses broke through thin ice, splashing in the shallows until they clambered up the river's bank on the far side. Kill Creek, the next ford, was almost dry. For the two Quaker farmers, this was their first excursion across the Territorial line; they seemed innocent of the possibility of violence. The other men, older, had been on previous raids into Missouri, targeting farmers who owned slaves. They were eager, self-assured, and boisterous about the success of prior raids.

The men camped at dusk in woods remote from any farmhouse. Trees and brush hid the yellow light of the campfire from the road. The next morning, they started early, resting the horses in late afternoon not far from their destination. Then they followed a lightly traveled road toward the Walker farm.

Crystals of white frost capped wagon ruts and hoof marks frozen in the black soil. The winter sun, blood red, clung to the western sky, but would soon be gone. Scarlet tinged the gray fields and stark trees.

A mile short of their destination, the band of men turned off the road and rode into a grove of trees, where they dismounted. By agreement, Will continued on alone. He told them he'd alert the slaves to their coming, so they could prepare to flee.

Will reined his horse to a walk when he reached the gate to Walker's farm. Barns loomed black against the scarlet sky. Horses stabled nearby moved restlessly in their stalls, and whinnied with the approach of the horseman. Light from oil lamps in the slave cabins flickered from the windows.

As Will approached the house, the door in the main house opened, briefly splashing light onto the covered porch. A man stepped outside and closed the door behind him, standing close to the wall of the house, partly concealed in the shadows. In the crook of his arm he held a musket, loaded with buckshot, instantly available but not intimidating to a friend.

"Mr. Walker, sir, is that you?" Will called out, just loud enough for the man on the porch to hear him. "My name's William Quantrill. I'm the one who stayed with Marcus Gill last winter. Over near New Santa Fe." Will remained on his horse. "He told me that you and he knew each other."

Silence. Then Morgan Walker said, "I remember the name." He stepped closer to the railing along the front of the porch, but remained indistinct in the dark. "What's Gill's oldest daughter's name?"

"That would be Leah, Mr. Walker."

"Right. Leah. She and my daughter met in Independence last year."

"Leah and I was friends, when I stayed with the family.

She's a mighty fine woman."

"What's your business, Mr. Quantrill?"

Dismounting from his horse, Will grasped the bridle's bit in his hand, up close to the horse's muzzle, and walked toward the man standing in the deep shadow at the top of the steps. They conversed for a few minutes in low tones. Satisfied, Will mounted his horse and headed back down the road from which he'd come.

Riding up to the five raiders waiting for him under the trees, he said, "They'll be ready for us. And those slaves sure were glad to hear we're coming to free them. Makes me feel right good about what we're doing."

One of the men asked if anyone saw him. "Don't think so. Lights were on in the house, but there wasn't a sign of anybody outside. Everything looked quiet. I think they must be at supper."

Will pulled the rifle out of the leather ring on his saddle, checked the load, then slipped the weapon back into its ring. "You, Lipsey, and Charlie Ball, when we get there, go with me up to the house. Ed Morrison, I want you to wait outside, in the front yard. Keep an eye on the road." The men nodded. "Albert Southwick, you go to the barn and pick out the horses we'll want to take with us. Johnny Dean, you decide which Negroes we want, and get a wagon ready to haul 'em." Johnny nodded. "If we have to kill the rebels, we can stay the night in their house and start early tomorrow. I'd rather do that, anyway, than head out tonight."

Will turned his horse out onto the road. The men followed, riding bunched together in an easy canter. White breath-clouds whipped away from the horses' nostrils in the sharp air. Will carried two pistols at his waist, Colt Model 1851 revolvers, .36 caliber. A third rested in the leather saddlebag. If there were a lot of shooting, there'd be no time to reload.

Light shone from the windows as they reined the horses to a walk and cautiously approached the house. Will and three of the men dismounted and tied the reins to a tree some distance back. Southwick slid off his horse and led it toward the barn. Johnny Dean rode on in the direction of the slave cabins.

When Will and the two other men mounted the porch steps, Charlie Ball fell back a little, and cupped the rifle in his right arm. Will pulled one of the pistols out of his belt and knocked at the door. Morgan Walker opened it, peered at the strangers, and asked who they were and what they wanted. Brushing him aside, Will entered the house, a pistol now in each hand. Lipsey went next, Charlie Ball behind him.

"We've come to take your slaves with us to Kansas," Will said brazenly. "We also want your horses and mules and what money you got in the house."

Morgan Walker replied firmly, "If my Negroes want to go to Kansas, they are at liberty to do so. But I don't see any reason why those who don't want to go should be forced to leave." Looking hard at Will, he added, "I don't think you should take any of my stock. They won't be worth much by the time you get 'em all the way over into Kansas."

As Walker protested, Will stepped farther into the room, a little to one side of Lipsey and Charlie Ball, who stood just inside the door. With an eye on the open doors leading into other rooms, he held both guns thrust out before him, ready to fire.

When Walker said, "Besides, I don't have much money here in the house—" Will spun around and fired a single shot at close range into Lipsey's head. Lipsey dropped to the floor, dead. Will immediately turned to fire at Charlie Ball, but an unseen man suddenly stepped through the door of an adjoining room, pistol raised at shoulder height, and fired at Charlie. Turning in reflex at the sound of the first shot to escape toward the open door, Charlie was struck in the shoulder instead of the chest. He fell back against the wall, regained his balance, and ran outside. Clutching his shoulder, he swung his legs over the porch rail and disappeared.

Hearing shots fired from inside, and seeing Charlie leap from the porch, Ed Morrison raced for the horses, a pistol in one hand. From the direction of the road, muzzle blasts nearby shattered the air, but missed him. Morrison grabbed the reins of his horse and fired back blindly at the unseen gunmen. With access to the road closed off, he jumped onto his horse and made for a stand of woods east of the house. Albert Southwick, waiting in the barn, heard the gunfire and saw Morrison fleeing for the woods. He climbed on his horse and galloped through the open barn door. Johnny Dean leaped onto his horse, tied up near the slave cabins, and rode off, lashing the animal for greater speed. He soon disappeared into a cornfield.

Back at the house, Will walked out onto the porch and into the shadows along one wall, still grasping a pistol in each hand. He peered out into the yard, searching for the source of the gunfire. Seeing two strangers approaching the house from out of the dark, each carrying a rifle, he dodged behind a column and raised his guns.

"Hold up, Quantrill!" Morgan Walker shouted from the door. "Those men are mine. I had them staked out behind the smokehouse."

Walker stepped back into the front room, where gunpowder smoke hung pungent in the air. Calling to his son, Andrew, to give him a hand, they picked up the body of Lipsey by its feet, dragged it through the open door, and laid the body on the wood floor near the far railing where the blood could drain off the edge onto the ground.

Will looked down at the dead man, one of whose arms lay flung to one side. With the toe of his boot, Will pushed the arm up against the man's body. "That should learn you something," he said.

"Andrew," Morgan Walker said, "get this body out to the tool shed, and cover it up. Tomorrow, have some men put it in a wagon and haul it off into the timber, back in that area where the brambles are taking over. Bury it there, so nobody's likely to stumble across it."

Turning to Will, Morgan Walker offered his hand. "We're grateful for what you done, Mr. Quantrill, warning us about the raid. Five men might have been too much for us to handle, not knowing they were coming. Stay the night, and in the morning, as soon as it's light, we'll look for the two that ran off. One of them being wounded, I don't think they'll get far."

Will nodded. "I want to finish what I started. No sense their getting away."

Morgan Walker was up and dressed before daylight. With his son and one of the men he'd staked out the night before, and with Will, they set out on horseback before breakfast to track down the remaining raiders. A Negro field worker told Morgan Walker he'd seen two men go into the woods near the creek. Because Charlie Ball was wounded, Walker doubted the men could move very fast. He was right. The hunters came upon their quarries by mid-morning. They sighted them concealed in the brush, lying flat on the ground alongside a log for cover.

The four men stealthily approached the hiding place. Ed Morrison, awakened from a light sleep by the cracking of a dry stick, rose to his knees, cautiously looking around. As he reached for his pistols, Morgan Walker knocked him to the ground with a blast of buckshot in the chest.

Charlie Ball struggled to rise up on his elbow, peering over the top of the log. His jacket was splotched with blood, and he shivered from the fever that had come on during the night. Shaking, he held a pistol in his good hand, but before he could get off a shot, Andrew fired at close range with a rifle, killing him instantly, the lead doubling Charlie over onto his back. Will stood by, his weapon at the ready, but did not fire a shot.

Morgan Walker sent his son to get some slaves and shovels. Meanwhile, the bodies were stripped of anything that might identify them. Clothes, boots, hats, leather belts were burned. Andrew Walker took a pocket watch and a miniature portrait locket from one of the bodies, to be disposed of elsewhere. If by chance the bodies were someday discovered, Walker wanted nothing that might identify them.

When the slaves arrived, they dug a common grave only yards from where the men had died, and deep enough that animals wouldn't dig at the buried bodies. The dead men were dumped into the cavity and the earth shoveled in, then spread with debris from the forest floor. In the silence, as the men stood back to look at the camouflaged burial site, it was as if the raiders had never crossed into Missouri.

Morgan Walker urged Will to stay for the noon meal with him and his family. At the table, Will related some of his exploits in Kansas, relishing the approval he got from his host. When Walker asked Will who the men from Kansas were, and why he had led them into a trap, Will smiled and replied only that he held a grudge against them, that he was righting a wrong inflicted on him and his family. Walker did not pursue the question further, respecting the younger man's right to keep such matters to himself.

That same afternoon, Will left the Walker farm astride a fine new horse with a hundred dollars cash in his pocket, gifts from Morgan Walker.

A week later, Marcus Gill read in *The Independence Democrat* a sympathetic account of the incident at Morgan Walker's farm. Will was not identified by name, nor did the article give the names of the men who had died in the attempted raid. But the journalist wrote that "One of the party, whom we understand had joined Montgomery's band for the purpose of being revenged upon by the death of his brother who had been killed by them," had set up the plan to warn the Walkers in advance of the raid, thereby setting a trap for the men who rode with him.

Marcus speculated it might have been Will who led the raiders. Once, when Will had asked him about his experiences in the Kentucky militia, Marcus had told Will of a similar episode of which he had knowledge, cautioning Will to avoid joining up with men he didn't know if his life might be dependent on them. Will seemed to take a particular interest in the story, nodding his head in agreement that one needed to be wary.

Marcus also surmised that Montgomery, a known organizer of anti-slavery raids launched from Lawrence, probably had nothing to do with the raid on Walker's farm, but that Will had planted the notion to add excitement to his feat, to make himself appear more of a hero. When Marcus showed the newspaper article to Mary Jane, she asked, "Did Will have a brother? I don't think he ever mentioned it to me."

"He once told me that he'd had a younger brother who also came out with him from Ohio," Marcus said. "He claimed that his brother and another man were camped out one night on the prairie west of Lawrence, looking after some cattle, when a band of Montgomery's raiders surprised them in their sleep and shot them dead."

"Oh, no," Mary Jane exclaimed, "what a horrible thing to have happen."

"I don't know," Marcus said, shaking his head. "I'm not sure it ever did. Will never spoke of his brother again. In fact, another time he lamented the fact that he was the only son his mother ever had, and he worried about how she would get along if he got killed someday."

"That's strange," Mary Jane said, then paused, thinking back to the conversations at the supper table when Will had lived with them. "But Will did seem to have a need to make things into something bigger than they were."

"I know, but I placed a lot of confidence in him. I still do –he undoubtedly saved my life, that day at the creek–and I know that Leah was real taken with him, when he stayed with us last winter. But Will has something deep inside, driving him so strong he won't be able to let go, should he ever have to. Like being on a runaway horse."

Mary Jane nodded. "I'm just glad the Noland boy has taken such an interest in Leah, and she seems to be feeling the same way about him. But I know she sometimes thinks about Will. Now and then she asks whether we've heard anything about him."

"Yes, I thought that was maybe the way things were. Well, we'll just have to wait to see what happens."

Marcus felt troubled. He couldn't understand why Will had not been in contact with them following the months he had lived in their house, during which he had seemed almost a part of the family. Why hadn't he at least written or sent a message? He must have known that they would have been concerned about him. Marcus was also annoyed that Will appeared to be inconsiderate of Leah's feelings for him. Perhaps Will wasn't all that Marcus had come to believe he was.

10

After the election of Lincoln in November, and the dramatic filling of seats with new members in state legislatures critically important to abolishing slavery, the country now waited to see how the new president would carry out the act. The inauguration of Lincoln, however, would not take place until March 4, almost four months after the election.

Would the country become even more divided during the transition from Buchanan to Lincoln? Already, warlike events were taking place. Confederate troops were being organized and armed. Newspapers reported that commanders of Union forts in states such as Texas, a slave state, were surrendering the military installations to the Confederate government without confrontation. Louisiana officials reached their hands into the United States mint in New Orleans and delivered $500,000 in federal funds to the Confederacy. Well before Lincoln's inauguration, it was becoming obvious that determined leaders in the South would not be deterred by the election of a president whose party was committed to the elimination of slavery.

Curiously, Lincoln remained all this time in Springfield, Illinois, drafting his inaugural address. He also called on friends, talked with hundreds of applicants hoping for appointments in the government, and hired two secretaries to sort and answer letters from job seekers. He assured his law partner that he would be back practicing law after leaving office.

Forming his cabinet, Lincoln designated William Seward, a former party rival but a powerful leader in the fledgling Republican organization, for secretary of state. Seward urged Lincoln to come to Washington to begin forging his new government. But threats on Lincoln's life were frequent. In the election's aftermath, deep anger prevailed among those not willing to give up slavery.

So Lincoln took precautions, among them delaying his arrival in the capital city. He seemed content to let Seward, an ambitious, action-driven spokesman for the administration, speak on his behalf.

Marcus faced each day wondering what steps the new administration would take on slavery. Contradictions were many. It was reported that Lincoln had forwarded a proposal to Seward for a constitutional amendment requiring Congress to leave slavery undisturbed in those states where it existed. But the same proposal included an amendment to the fugitive slave law that would give runaway slaves the right to a jury trial. Meanwhile, the government continued to support the lawful return of fugitive slaves to their owners.

Seward himself held out to Southern states that a compromise on slavery might still be reached. Newspaper editors in the South, however, suspicious of Seward, deduced that he was stalling for time, hoping that secessionist fervor would fade. But as those Southern states that had announced secession hastily prepared to fight, if necessary, to preserve their Constitutional rights and to seek redress for their grievances, the conflicting pronouncements only heightened their fervor.

During the last ten days of December, while Lincoln remained in Springfield, legislators of seven Southern states gathered in Montgomery, Alabama, and approved directives for secession. Marcus was encouraged; at last, Southerners were acting forcefully on their convictions. But he then learned that Virginia, a leader among the Southern states, defeated delegates favoring secession. Virginia would remain in the Union for now. Was the coalition beginning to fall apart?

More bad news followed. Voters in Tennessee refused to call a convention to consider secession. Arkansas then rejected convention candidates who favored secession. North Carolina was next, refusing to hold a convention sought by secessionists. Kentucky stayed with the Union. This angered Marcus, that the Southern state in which both he and Lincoln were born would abandon other slave states. The South appeared divided even against itself. Marcus could not understand why the Southern states could not unite.

As the inauguration date crept closer, fears mounted. What acts would this new president take, once in office? But Lincoln reassured them, saying that he would enforce the fugitive slave law, and that he would deliver protection of property rights provided by the Constitution, one of which was the right to own slaves. He would carry out what the

Constitution called for, he insisted, whether he personally approved or not.

Lincoln also asserted that the Union could not be lawfully divided, that no state had the right to leave it. If a state seceded, that would be an unlawful act, and he was determined to uphold the law. His message on that was clear and unmistakable.

It was not until late February, more than three months after his election, when Lincoln left Springfield and traveled to Washington. Heeding advice from his advisors, he arrived quietly, without public celebration, so as not to draw attention from those who might harm him. On March 4, he was sworn in as president, and gave the speech on which he had worked for many weeks. He asked the country to be calm, and said that the momentous issue of civil war confronted them all. The government would not assail–the very word he used–would not assail the South if the Union itself was not assailed, but both North and South must recognize that he had taken a solemn oath to preserve, protect, and defend the Union.

The day after his inaugural, Lincoln heard from the Union commander at Fort Sumter in Charleston Harbor that food and supplies were running out and that he needed 20,000 men to protect the fort against the Confederates. But Lincoln was not ready for an event that might catapult the nation into war. Furthermore, his military leader, Gen. Winfield Scott, cautioned that the Union army could not reinforce Fort Sumter for many months.

Seward favored abandoning Fort Sumter, and he urged patience, saying that in time, the rebelling states would return to the Union. Most of the country knew that Fort Sumter, deep in the Confederacy, was vulnerable. Its fate overshadowed all other concerns, and was commonly discussed everywhere. The fort was like a linchpin which, if it fell, would cause the wheel to spin off its axle. Lincoln steadfastly believed that Unionists in the South outnumbered those who favored secession. It seemed inconceivable to him that the South would precipitate civil war.

It was as if the eight remaining slaveholding states held the Union hostage. Lincoln feared that if the Union attacked Confederates in South Carolina, then Virginia, for whom Fort Sumter's strategic location was critical to its own welfare, would join the Confederacy. Lincoln was adamant that he would not give up Fort Sumter as a Union stronghold.

The decision, however, of whether to defend Fort Sumter by attacking with military force in South Carolina, was taken out of his hands. Jefferson Davis, president of the Confederacy, chose to launch the naval attack on the fort, saving Lincoln from assailing the South. On April 12, 1861, Confederate warships fired their cannons on Fort Sumter. After two days of siege, the fort was theirs.

Marcus knew that war would now be declared, and felt the world closing in. Like invaders, events beyond his control pounded on his door and forced their way into his home, requiring him to confront the likelihood of further assaults on him and his family. Was he a fool to stay, was he risking the lives of his family? He could not decide. But he would not give up.

11

Eight days before the fall of Sumter, Leah married Jesse Noland. The wedding took place in her father's house. Jesse was twenty-six, Leah seventeen. Their families and friends gathered in the parlor in mid-afternoon. Leah and Jesse stood in front of the massive stone hearth while the preacher, his back to the fire, faced them, and read the marriage vows. Leah still had heard nothing from Will since he rode off for Lawrence and had decided she never would.

Jesse's parents had a fine house in Independence. They believed in the right to own slaves. When Marcus asked Jesse's father whether he would remain in Independence if war broke out, he replied that he would, even though his son was eager to join the Confederate Army. After all, Independence was his home. His largest concern was whether, as a known Southerner, his job in county government might be threatened. But he assured Marcus that he and his wife welcomed Leah into their family, and they were glad that the young couple would be living with them.

A few days later, Marcus received a letter from his oldest son, Enoch, living in Texas. He had married a girl whose family had been neighbors in Kentucky. Enoch and his new wife had joined his wife's family when they moved west to Texas.

"Regretfully, you are located in the worst possible place," he wrote. "Those merciless raiders in Kansas will not stop. They will steal your property and very possibly harm you. And now that we're at war, you and Mama will be in great peril. Come to Texas. We've seceded, and you'll be far safer here. "

Marcus anguished over what to do. Outwardly, he went about managing the farm with Jed at his side. They both continued carrying firearms whenever they went out into the fields, away from the house. The slaves seemed apprehensive; Marcus felt that they were watching him whenever he rode by or stopped to talk with Jed. Marcus assumed that Millie and the house servants passed along to other slaves any conversation they overheard. The slaves must have had some awareness of unfolding events, but Marcus did not consider it further; he was too absorbed with the safety of his family and the operation of the farm.

A few nights later, shortly before midnight, Mary Jane awakened. The room was cold. She got out of bed and walked over to the open window to close it. The scent of freshly mowed hay in a nearby pasture drifted into the room.

To the east, she saw a red glow low on the horizon. At first it looked as if the sun was edging upward. Then she turned, and shook Marcus. Waking, he instinctively reached for the revolver on a bedside table.

"No," Mary Jane said, "not that. It's a fire. Look, over there."

Even at that distance, he could make out tongues of flame, pulsing like fanned coals in a kiln.

"Carter Johnson's?" Mary Jane asked.

"Could be. The raiders have been active in that part of the county."

"What can we do?"

"Nothing, it's too far, and too late to help," Marcus said. "There's no way to stop a fire like that. But I'll ride over after daybreak, and see what they might need." He shivered, and wrapped his arms around his body. "If it's the house, and not one of the barns, they'll need a place to live until they can get it rebuilt. Farmers nearby will help out."

Mary Jane went back to bed. Marcus lay down beside her, both unable to sleep.

"Marcus, what are we going to do? I mean, what are we going to do about staying here, with the war going on?"

He put his arm around her, and she lay her head against his chest. "I've been thinking about that, most all the time. But I didn't want to worry you anymore than you already were."

"Can we go someplace else? Until the fighting's over?"

"I'd sure hate to walk away and leave the place. Jed could stay here, look after things, but there's very little one man can do to keep up the place like it should be. And if raiders show up, he'd best hide until they're gone. And they probably will come."

"Why do you think that?" Mary Jane asked.

"Word will get around as soon as we're gone that the house is empty, that there's only one man around. When we come back, we could find all the buildings burned to the ground."

"But you've worked so hard to build up the farm."

"And they'd likely as not kill Jed, if they found him alone."

Marcus stared up at the ceiling. The walnut planks were barely visible in the darkness, yet he remembered, seven years ago now, watching them being sawed from a great tree felled in the timber near the creek bank, and hauled by a pair of mules to the site of his new house.

"I think that you, or me, or any of us could be shot and killed, Mary Jane. In war, anything can happen. It's not only the raiders who can harm us. There'll be Union troops. And the state militia. They'll look at us as the enemy. We're Southerners, and we own slaves."

"Even though you're not in the army? Even though you're not fighting?"

"Yes, it can happen. A commander can't always control his troops, especially when they're spread out. Patrols, just six or eight men. They're on their own, can do what they want, whatever they can get away with."

"So Union soldiers might be just as bad as the guerrillas?"

"That's always a possibility. Like I said, we're the enemy."

"But you're not a soldier," Mary Jane said again. "You're not in the Confederate Army."

"They might not see it that way. And there's the bushwhackers. They're better organized now, itching for a fight whenever they can find guerrillas or someone they think is abolitionist. That means trouble can explode just about anywhere."

Mary Jane nodded. "The Nolands told Leah they know of several gangs in the county. Jesse is pleased. He figures they're out to help people like us, and they'll give raiders as much trouble as they cause."

"I'm thinking more about military fighting, with troops, and where it might take place. You never know ahead of time. But there's no reason why it can't be right here in Jackson County. There could be a battle right here on the farm anywhere, anytime."

Marcus saw in his mind companies of uniformed soldiers advancing across his fields and pastures, shouting, firing rifles amidst clouds of gunpowder smoke, and tearing down rail fences to remove obstructions to their advance. He saw artillery hauled by struggling horses, soldiers setting up cannons to fire, and explosions from opposing artillery demolishing his house, destroying his barns, erupting like geysers in the fields and tearing raw holes in the earth. He saw decaying carcasses of livestock, corpses of soldiers sprawled in his pastures, heard cries of wounded and dying men, and saw the thrashing of cavalry horses felled by gunfire. As a boy, his grandfather had told him vivid stories about the Revolutionary War, when he had fought as a cavalry captain. Those tales had stayed with him, enhanced by his own experiences.

"There's something else," he said. "The military road south from Leavenworth is just to the west, not far from us."

"What does that mean?"

"Armies depend on military roads to move troops and artillery and supplies. Both sides can use them. Depends on who has control at any one time. Because of their size, armies stretch out some distance on either side of the road. They also scavenge for food and horses, mules, wagons, whatever they need, wherever they go."

"Then Enoch was right," Mary Jane said. "We're caught in the middle."

"Others are, too. We wouldn't be the only victims. But if

we leave, we ought to do it soon. As soon as we can get ready."

"But, Marcus—" Mary Jane stopped, then said, "Should we go to Texas? And why don't we have more time? To get ready?"

"Raiders will step up their activities, now that war's been declared. There will be more gangs, like packs of dogs, yelping and fighting anyone they run up against. Wild dogs."

"And Texas? Should we go?"

"It's a long trip. Twenty miles a day, down through Oklahoma, about the best we could do. It would take three weeks, maybe longer. Oxen would haul the wagons. They're slow, but they're stronger than mules." Marcus began to visualize how they might do it, if they went. "The longer we wait, the more likely it is there'll be fighting along the way. Federal troops will be watching the roads."

"But so soon?" Mary Jane asked again.

"True, it takes time for armies to build up their strength, to where they're ready to fight. States like the Carolinas, Virginia, Georgia, that's where the first battles will be fought. But before long, fighting will likely get to Missouri and Arkansas. Truth is, I'd like to get back down to the South. We'd be with our kind of people."

"So shouldn't we have plenty of time to do that?"

"No, because troops will be sent here as soon as they can. Both sides will be angling early on to control the rivers. That's the fastest way to transport men and supplies. The longer we wait, the more chance that we'll be stopped on the way by Union troops. They'll steal our wagons and everything we have. We might be harmed, too. Anything can happen when there's fighting all around."

Mary Jane was silent. Then she said, "I've been thinking

about Leah, Marcus. Jesse told her he's leaving next week to go South, to enlist in the Southern army. Should we take Leah with us?"

"If she can stay on with the Nolands, I think that might be best. They'll be glad to have her. Independence is a big enough town, I think she'd be safe, even if Union troops come in. Many of the folks there side with the Union, but Southern families shouldn't be harmed as long as they don't get caught helping Confederates or bushwhackers."

As they talked it out, Marcus began to accept the growing inevitability of their leaving the farm. He thought the war might not last long, that the federal government would relent when they realized how determined the South was to retain their rights. Economic strength in the Northern states was greater than in the South, he realized, but the resolve of Southerners not to be intimidated was powerful. He and Mary Jane would probably be back home within a year, he figured, maybe sooner. Meanwhile, his family would likely be safer in Texas, away from the pillaging and guns of the Kansas raiders.

"I've been thinking that I should try to get in touch with Will," Marcus said. "I'd feel a lot better with someone like him traveling with us, at least until we got through Oklahoma Territory. We need another man who's good with a gun, knows what to look out for, and knows how to fight."

"Since Leah won't be with us," Mary Jane said, "I think you're right. Will respects you and he just might want to be doing something like that. He likes excitement, and likes being in the midst of things that show how good he is."

"Jesse's family might know where Will could be found. I'll maybe ride on into Independence, after I leave the Johnsons, and see what I can find out about him."

For a few moments, neither spoke. Then Mary Jane asked, "How long will it take for us to get ready to leave?"

"I'll have to buy some wagons. I want to take as much of our furniture, our household things, as we can. With no one living in the house, whatever we leave won't be here when we get back, even if the house isn't burned."

"I can start packing up things right away. What about the slaves? Will we take them with us?"

"Texas is a slave state, of course," Marcus replied, "so we could. Besides, we'll need them when we come home, to put the place back in shape. The women slaves could ride on top of the wagons. The men could ride the horses and mules we'd take with us."

"I can't imagine leaving Millie behind," Mary Jane said. "What would she do if we did?"

"I'm not sure. Follow the roads to Lawrence, maybe. Then someplace farther north, after that."

"You need to write Turner, Marcus. To tell him to come home."

"Yes, you're right. I'll do that directly after I get back from the Walkers. And you write Enoch, to tell him we're coming."

Marcus had slept only a short time before Mary Jane awakened him again; it was time to ride to Carter Johnson's to see what he could do to help.

The next evening, after supper, Marcus went alone to the place where his infant son lay buried. It was four years ago that the boy had died. At the gravesite he found a sprig of dogwood, lying atop the grave, the edges of the fragile white petals already turning brown. Mary Jane must have placed it there earlier in the day.

His mind flooded with many thoughts, Marcus stood for a time, unmoving. Then he walked over to Jim's grave, in a corner of the small plot, marked by a rough piece of uncut stone picked up from the creek bed. On one irregular side, the name "Jim" had been scratched, as if with the point of a nail, and the month and year of his death. The letters and numerals were irregular, and already eroding in the soft, sand-colored stone.

At that moment, an image of Effie flashed into his mind. She was standing across from him, on the other side of Jim's grave, as she had the day her husband was buried. Marcus saw clearly her anguished face. He saw the tears on her cheeks and her hands clenched tightly at her breast. Marcus again felt her eyes looking through him and beyond, as if fixed on something she sought, something beyond him from which she was unwilling to turn away.

How, he asked himself, how had he been able to put the old slave out of his mind during those many years since he had been a boy? How could he have forgotten the man who had patiently shown him how to grasp the worn, smooth handle of the great scythe, how to swing it from one side to the other, his whole, young body moving with it? He had not often seen Jim since and seldom to speak to, Marcus realized. The slave had become only one of many working in the fields, indistinguishable at that distance.

Marcus felt a sudden rush of tenderness for the old man. He was also deeply sad the slave was now dead. Yes, the old man had belonged to him, had been his property. His father had bought Jim, and given Jim to his son, Marcus. No law-ful person would have contested his right to use the slave however he wished. But now a strange feeling distorted that logical fact.

Gradually he began to understand why the sight of the old man lying in his bed had disturbed him so profoundly. He remembered the slave's wasted body, the hair gone almost white. He remembered that the old man, although only momentarily able to recognize his master, had brightened when he saw his face. Marcus had found himself at that moment thinking of Jim as someone who had been a part of his own early life, someone important to him in those days of childhood, as something, someone, other than property.

So Marcus had not told Mary Jane that he had been thinking about offering his slaves freedom. The more Marcus considered the alternative, the more unsure he became of his judgment. Others would think he had lost his senses. Perhaps he had; the pressures from all sides were great. Yet he continued to weigh the possibility in his mind, as well as to consider the great financial loss that giving up his slaves would mean.

12

Turner returned from the university as soon as he received the letter from his father asking him to come home. Marcus and Jed then rode into Westport, leaving Turner and the field foreman to watch out for any raiders who might appear.

Marcus bought five wagons, similar to those used by traders who traveled to Santa Fe, laden with goods to sell or exchange for merchandise to sell when the wagons returned to Missouri. These wagons had iron-shod wooden wheels higher than a horse's back, and wagon beds so deep that the head of a tall man standing inside was barely visible over the sides. He also bought forty head of oxen, enough for four yokes hitched to each wagon. When loaded with household furnishings, bedding, a month's supply of food and grain, kegs of well water, farming implements, bales of hay, and other possessions, each wagon would weigh more than three tons.

Marcus had paid for his purchases and was about ready
to leave the provisioner's store when he heard a voice say,
"Colonel Gill, heard you were looking for me."

Standing in the door was Will, a wide grin on his face. He
looked fit, was dressed in new clothes, and wore two revolvers in holsters at his waist. A long feather stuck in his hat-
band rose jauntily above the crown.

Marcus was glad to see him, and they walked out onto
the street together. Will asked about the family, although he
seemed to avoid referring to Leah by name. Marcus told
him that Leah was newly married, one of the Nolands in
Independence. Will said he'd heard that, and wished her
well. Marcus searched Will's face for some sign of emotion,
of regret, but saw nothing.

Marcus then explained that he was taking his family to
Texas, that they would be leaving in just a few days.

"I'd like to hire you to go with us, Will," Marcus said.
"You saved my life once. I don't expect to call on you to do
that again, but I need you, in case we run into trouble. You're
the best I know. I hope you'll agree to go with us. You can
come back after we get to Fayette County, if you like. That's
west of the town of Houston. Or you'd be welcome to stay
on with us. It would be up to you."

Will made up his mind quickly. "I'd like to go with you.
Haven't never been to Texas. Fact is, I'd enjoy doing something like that right at this time."

Marcus reached out his hand. Will shook it, and prom-
ised he'd be at the farm early in the morning on the day
they'd be leaving.

The departure day set, much now needed to be done.
The family worked alongside the slaves, preparing to load

the huge wagons with all they'd be taking with them. The leather-bound Bible was placed inside the lacquered-wood container that once held Mary Jane's silver place settings, and wrapped in a blanket, bound with twine. Gunnysacks stuffed with straw were used to pack china, the glass globes of coal-oil lamps, and other easily broken possessions. Furniture was protected by bedding not needed until they arrived in Texas, and then hauled up into a wagon. Clothing was carefully folded and laid in leather trunks.

Mary Jane was determined to leave nothing behind that might be vandalized or stolen. The possibility that men like Slater and his raiders could break open the door and ransack her home, perhaps set it afire in anger when they found little left to plunder, drove her to give away to neighbors, or lend for safekeeping, three chests of drawers, a dressing table, the iron range, and other pieces of furniture they decided not to take with them.

Under Jed's instructions, slaves loaded hand tools from the barn into one of the wagons, together with bales of hay to feed the horses and mules they were taking with them, if good forage could not be found along the way. Marcus reasoned that livestock would become more valuable as the war progressed; that he'd get a better price in Texas, if he had to sell his livestock, than he could now at markets in Westport or Independence.

Marcus waited to execute his plan until the next-to-last day before they would leave. Even Jed did not know the decision he had been contemplating for days. Marcus had discussed it with Mary Jane, but waited until late that afternoon to tell the older children.

After supper, he instructed Jed to assemble the slaves outside their cabins. The April air, unusually warm, already smelled of summer: the heavy scent of verdant pastures, and the pungent odor of hog pens and of cattle, moving restlessly nearby in a corral.

The slaves stood bunched together by families, or stood singly a little apart from the others, if they were without family. Several women held infants in their arms. Other children stood next to their parents; a few, very small, clung to a hand or a leg. They were silent, even the younger children, as if sensing something of which they should be afraid.

Marcus saw Effie standing to one side, alone. She seemed to have aged, her hair more gray, her body more bent than he had remembered. She looked at him for a sign, any sign that might indicate what was happening; finding none, she shifted her gaze toward the woods in the distance, as if disdainful of whatever he might do.

The men, who wore their hats from the fields, despite the evening's warmth, stood quietly. No one talked. Marcus sensed the apprehension displayed by the stiff postures, the arms hanging loosely at their sides, the eyes staring at him, or turned downward, waiting, as if afraid to face him.

Marcus knew that what he would say might not be easily apprehended. So he began slowly.

First, he acknowledged that some of them had made the journey with him from Kentucky, to this new land; that others he had bought after he'd arrived in Missouri. He told them that war had begun; that Southerners like himself were not willing to give up slavery. They were willing to fight to uphold federal and state laws in which they believed. He said that even though Missouri permitted slavery, the state government had decided not to secede, but to stay with the Union, taking sides with those opposed to slavery. He regretted this decision, he told them, because there were many

Southerners like himself who had come west to build a new
life, and they felt betrayed by their government.

Marcus wondered how much the slaves understood. What
did they know about the laws of which he spoke, the government in Washington? Never in the past would he have
undertaken to talk to them as he was now doing. But because of what he was about to say, he felt compelled to ex-
plain what was happening in their lives as well as his own.

He had decided to take his family to Texas, he told them.
They knew this, because they had been helping in prepara-
tions to leave. Fighting would possibly take place nearby,
even on his own land, he explained, perhaps where they
now stood; no one could know before it happened. There
would be much danger, if they remained where they were.

Watching their faces, Marcus saw no changes in expres-
sions, no sign that they comprehended what he was telling
them. He wasn't sure that they did. After all, until now there
had been no decisions for them to make.

His voice becoming firm, Marcus said that he was offering them their freedom. Whoever chose to be free, he would
free them before he left for Texas. Those who decided to
remain with him he would take with him, where they would
remain with his family.

It was as if he had spoken in a strange language whose
sounds reached their ears, but whose meaning remained a
mystery. The faces before him were either blank or reflected
emotions Marcus could not recognize.

More gently, Marcus repeated what he had just said, phras-
ing the message in simplest terms.

In a matter of such great import, who would not have
asked that the message be repeated? He added that they
would have until daybreak tomorrow morning to decide.

Jed would call them together again at that time. Those who chose freedom would be given a letter of manumission. Marcus explained that this was a written statement, signed by him, stating that he had freed the slave whose name was written on the paper.

Where could they go? For a few days, Marcus said, they could stay in their cabins, if they wished. But it would be best for them if they left right away. Slave owners who remained in the county might not honor the freedom he had granted them. Also, there were renegades who might harm them, once they were out of his protection.

They could take with them whatever food they could carry. But soon after he and his family were gone, he said, he urged that they cross over into Kansas Territory and travel the roads northward to Leavenworth, where there was an Army fort. It would be dangerous for them even on the roads north, because actions of the Kansas guerrillas, while declaring that they wanted to free slaves, were unpredictable. He could not assure the slaves of their safety.

When Marcus concluded, he paused for a moment, as if about to say something more, but abruptly turned about and walked toward his house. Looking back over his shoulder, he saw that no one had moved. They stood where he had left them, as if the energy to move their limbs, to walk, had drained out of their bodies and flowed silently and unseen into the soil.

The next morning, Jed came to the house soon after daybreak. Marcus had not yet finished breakfast, but he had kept an eye out for Jed, and met him at the door.

Only Millie, Jed told him, another woman slave, and three of the older field hands had chosen to go with the family to

Texas. The rest had all said they wanted freedom.

For a moment, Marcus was angry. He had expected more. He had treated his slaves well, he felt. Most had been with him for years. Why so many would choose the hazards, the uncertain future of freedom, he could not understand.

"Well, then, that's the way it'll be," he said. "Give each slave, each family all the food they can carry."

"What about those staying?" Jed asked, tugging at his old hat. "What I mean is, those going with us? To Texas."

"Tell Millie and the other slave there'll be space in the wagons for them to take a few things, whatever's important to them. Take a look at what they want to take, and see where it'll best fit. The same for the men, although I doubt that they'll have much. Use your own judgment."

Jed nodded, and turned to leave.

"Come back in an hour," Marcus said. "I'll need you to give me the names of those leaving, so I can write out the releases. Then you can take their papers to them."

When Jed returned, Marcus led him into the parlor and sat down at his desk. Jed, who was unable to read or write, stood to his side. Marcus opened a drawer and took out sheets of blue-tinted writing paper. He folded each sheet over once, then again; and with the blade of a knife, cut the paper into four parts. Each quarter section of the page was all that was needed to write out the words: "I, Marcus Gill, on this 23rd day, April 1861, do hereby release and manumit for all time my slave . . . " and then fill in the slave's given name, the only name the slave was known by.

From memory, Jed spoke the names. In his mind he passed from one cabin to the next, now pushing the brim of his hat a little higher on his forehead, then giving it a tug to pull it back into place, as he said them aloud. One by one, waiting patiently until the colonel began a new slip of paper, Jed scrupulously accounted for every adult slave, the slave's wife, and each child, even infants. At the end of the simple, declarative sentence Marcus wrote on the tinted paper, he dropped a line and signed his name in flourishing script. When Marcus had finished, Jed asked him to say how many names there were. Marcus counted twenty-two, not including the five who would go with them to Texas. Jed nodded in agreement. The number was right.

That night, the night before they would set out, neither Marcus nor Mary Jane slept more than a few hours. Their bed had already been disassembled and loaded onto a wagon, so they stretched a blanket on the floor over cotton bags stuffed with straw. They would use the blanket and straw bags again, each night on the trail. The house, although nearly empty of possessions, seemed alive with both strange and accustomed noises, as if bewildered shapes were wandering restlessly about in confusion.

At dawn, a wagon train of formidable size began to assemble on the pasture north of the house. Herders responsible for getting the livestock to Texas separated Marcus's prize horses and Kentucky mules into manageable herds. The animals would follow behind the wagons, because of the dust they'd kick up and the manure droppings. The oxen, at pasture since they had been brought from Westport, were rounded up, preparatory to yoking them to the wagons. The hogs, sold to other farmers, were gone from their pens, as were the chickens from the coops, now eerily silent.

Will appeared early that morning, as he had said he would. When he knocked at the door, Mary Jane let him in, and asked if he'd had his breakfast. She was distant in her greeting, unforgiving for his failure to communicate with Leah after he'd left the family and gone to Lawrence.

Will said coffee would be just fine. The younger children, shy at first, were soon tagging after him, until Marcus told them to leave Will alone, that he had to get ready, too. Marcus saw that Will was in high spirits, excited at the prospect of being bound for Texas, and that he enthusiastically took to his role as protector of the family.

By mid-morning, all else was ready. It was time to yoke the oxen to the wagons.

Marcus mounted his dapple-gray gelding. The horse, sensing the excitement in the air, had to be kept under a tight rein. Sitting erect in the saddle, his face shadowed by the soft, floppy brim of his hat, Marcus rode up to the wagonmaster, astride a roan mare, and spoke quietly to him. The wagonmaster, hired in Westport to make the journey, was the most experienced Marcus could find. With sunburned face and a broad girth, the wagon master wore a brightly colored shirt, a hat drawn low on his head, neckerchief at the throat, high boots, and a revolver and long knife in his belt. At Marcus's words, he touched the brim of his hat, turned, and with his hands cupped to his mouth, called out: "Yoke up! Yoke up!", and then again, stretching the words into a prolonged cry, "Yo-o-o-ke up! Yo-o-o-ke up!"

The words sang out over the expanse of wagons and oxen, hanging suspended in the air before they were picked up and repeated by the bullwhackers, also hired out of Westport, who were standing ready. "Yoke up! Yoke up!" they shouted, like soldiers going into battle, and fell to the task of moving the placid, waiting oxen into massive wooden yokes, each connected to tongues fifty feet long, extending from the front of the wagons. The great beasts, prodded by the bullwhackers, ambled into their yokes as if to feed at a trough. Astonishingly, within a half-hour, the task was done.

On command from the wagonmaster, a bullwhacker standing to the left of the wheelers, the rear yoke on the first wagon, raised his arm, paused, and in a practiced motion, flung the tip of the long whip out and over the backs of the oxen, shouting "H-u-u-up! H-u-u-up!"

Like a gathering storm, energy and force rumbled out of the oxen's massive shoulders, their hooves pushed hard at the ground and the wheels of the wagons shuddered as the inertia of the great weight they bore was overcome, and the wheels turned slowly, slowly forward.

Marcus watched the proceedings, the expression on his face changing almost imperceptibly with the thoughts rushing through his head. Swallows, undeterred by the commotion, darted and plunged near the roofs of the barns, plucking insects out of the warm spring air. Split-rail fences marched evenly across the hills and valleys of his farm. Redbud again threw splashes of color along edges of the timber, beginning to green with the elegant lace of new foliage.

He gazed beyond his house to the cemetery, sketched against the sky, shielded by the black iron fence. A young oak tree, its bare branches only beginning to leaf out, stood like a ragged banner in a field of honor. In his mind, Marcus saw the slate headstone for his infant son, and the smaller, rough stone for Jim, side by side from so far.

He sat solidly on his horse, looking out over the fields, and again toward the house and barns. In the pasture between the slave cabins and the road leading north toward Westport, and then across into Kansas Territory, he saw the figures of his former slaves walking slowly, burdened with bundles of clothing and food. Hardly enough food to take them far, he conjectured, but he had done all he could.

At that distance, he did not recognize any one slave. They were indistinguishable, one from another, because of the shabby clothes they wore and because they faced away from him, toward uncertainty, toward a future they had chosen.

A future they had chosen. The unspoken words resounded in his mind as Marcus pulled hard on the reins, turned his horse about, and rode to catch up with the wagons.

Epilogue

Marcus Gill and his wife, Mary Jane, remained in Texas until the Civil War ended. That same year, 1865, they returned to Missouri, driving a small wagon containing whatever personal possessions the wagon would hold. Their two younger children, ages four and six, rode in the wagon behind the seat from which Marcus drove the team of mules. The three older children traveled in a second wagon, probably driven by Susan, seventeen, a younger sister of Leah.

Marcus had invested heavily in bonds issued by the Confederacy; and at the war's end, the bonds were worthless. When they reached the family farm in Jackson County, he found the house still standing, as well as some of the farm buildings, but the fences had been stolen for firewood, and the fields and pastures showed the neglect and ravages of the last four years.

He set about rebuilding, selling off some of the land when he found it was more than he could manage. Marcus and Mary Jane continued to live on the farm and work it until, at age sixty-nine, he divided up ownership of the property among their children. All five daughters who lived into adulthood had been married in the house Marcus Gill built, in front of the great stone hearth. Marcus and Mary Jane then moved to a small place near Plattsburg, in Clinton County, Missouri, about thirty miles north of the Missouri River, where they had recourse to the mineral springs located nearby.

Marcus Gill died only three years later, in 1886, at age seventy-two. Mary Jane lived until 1894; she, too, was seventy-two when she died. They are buried in the Gill family plot in Elmwood Cemetery in Kansas City, Missouri.

About a third of the original farm remained within the family of descendants of Susan Gill McGee, the second oldest daughter of Marcus and Mary Jane, until 1959, 105 years after the Gills came to Jackson County from Kentucky. By 1959, the property was within the city limits of Kansas City, Missouri. At that time, the remaining acreage was sold for residential development, although construction did not begin until twenty years later.

Today, a thirteen-acre public park with a small lake at 119th Terrace and Pennsylvania Street comprises a part of the original farm. In all directions, houses march in curving symmetry over the hills and valleys of what was once Marcus Gill's thousand acres. A limestone column bearing two bronze plaques recounts the history of the farm and those few events relating to the border conflict. The boundaries of the farm, when viewed today, were from State Line Road to Wornall Road on the east, and from about 116th Street

on the north to 121st Street on the south, two blocks north
of the street named Santa Fe Trail.

William Clarke Quantrill

Quantrill returned from Texas soon after he arrived there
with Marcus Gill and his family. He was restless, and wanted
to be back in Missouri, where he knew the action would be.

In August 1863, in the second year of the Civil War, William Clarke Quantrill carried out an act destined to give
him lasting notoriety. He led a band of nearly 450 men on a
raid of Lawrence, Kansas, seat of the abolitionist movement
in Kansas, in which his guerrillas slaughtered 144 civilians,
all men and boys, most unarmed. A sense of Southern gallantry kept the Quantrill raiders from harming women or
girls. Not a single guerrilla was killed.

The raid was partly in retaliation for the deaths a few days
earlier of five women and the severe injuries suffered by
other women, none more than twenty years of age. They
had been imprisoned by Union soldiers on the second floor
of a three-story brick building at 1409 Grand Avenue in
Kansas City, Missouri. The young women were suspected
of being spies for the Southern cause. A thirteen-year-old
girl, who had provoked one of the guards, had been shackled at the ankle to a twelve-pound ball. For reasons still de-
bated, the building trembled and collapsed with only a few
moments warning. The girl shackled at the ankle was among
those killed as the building disintegrated. At least eight of
the women who died or were critically injured were sisters
or cousins of men who rode as guerrillas with Quantrill.

General Thomas Ewing, Jr., the district commander of
the Union forces, and a man with huge political ambitions,
then compounded the anguish of the survivors of the vic-

tims killed in the building's collapse. He issued Order No. 10, which authorized the arrest of all men and women who knowingly and of their own volition assist and encourage the Southern guerrillas, and to remove them from their homes and families to a location outside the state of Missouri. Still stunned by the deaths of the young women only four days before, the guerrillas now knew that their family members risked being deported from Missouri with only those possessions they could carry with their hands, and with little money obtainable for their support.

From the viewpoint of Quantrill's raiders and Southern sympathizers, the Lawrence raid was a magnificent victory. They made off with 400 to 500 horses, terrorized all whom they encountered, left many buildings aflame, and stole vast amounts of loot. The raiders must have felt as if they had vindicated the deaths of their loved ones and had struck a great blow against the Union and the abolitionist cause. Sadly, their foes were only civilians little able to defend themselves, and not uniformed soldiers in the Union Army, not even Lane's or Montgomery's abolitionist raiders.

For the next year, Quantrill continued to stage daring raids and skirmishes. By October 1864, however, the tide began to turn. Confederate Gen. Sterling Price, a Missourian and leader of many excursions into the state against Union forces, was devastatingly defeated at a battle with Union forces under the command of Gen. James G. Blunt. Price's defeat demoralized troops in the Army of Missouri. Many soldiers deserted; they saw Price's defeat as the end of the war for Missouri Confederates.

Quantrill also read the signs. He and his men, about thirty in all, in December 1864 dressed themselves in Union uniforms and left Missouri for eastern Arkansas, then into Mississippi, Tennessee, and finally into southwestern Kentucky.

Still disguised, they duped Union loyalists into giving them provisions, and generally raised hell: robbing individuals, stealing horses, looting, and destroying property. Quantrill's ranks were gradually diminished in skirmishes when, their disguise uncovered, they had to shoot their way out and were killed or caught.

Although Robert E. Lee had surrendered almost 28,000 of his troops at Appomattox Courthouse on April 9, 1865, and was followed nine days later by Gen. J. E. Johnston, who surrendered another 31,000 soldiers, it was not until more than six weeks later, May 26th, that the last of the rebel troops gave up their arms.

Meanwhile, near the town of Taylorsville, on the Salt River in the southwest corner of Kentucky, a farmer named James H. Wakefield agreed to harbor Quantrill and his guerrillas when they needed a place from time to time to hide out. On May 10, 1865, Quantrill and twenty-one of his men, including several newcomers, arrived at the Wakefield farm.

The horse that Quantrill had ridden through many episodes of fighting, Old Charley, had been injured shortly before while being shoed, and was irredeemably crippled. Quantrill was dismayed, sensing that the loss of the horse which had carried him swiftly and without serious injury to either of them for so long, was a bad sign. Forced to find another mount, Quantrill borrowed a horse from a woman friend. Unfortunately, the animal had never been exposed to gunfire, and therefore not conditioned to battle. That proved to be a tragic flaw.

Apparently unknown to Quantrill, he and his gang were being pursued by a man named Edwin Terrell, a discharged Union soldier. Terrell was considered by many to be very dangerous and a reprehensible renegade. He had been hired in January by the commander of the Union garrison in Louisville, Kentucky, to hunt down Confederate guerrillas. When he wasn't specifically engaged in that pursuit, he and his gang robbed civilians, yet went without being apprehended. In early April 1865, despite such known nefarious activities, Terrell was instructed by the military commander of Kentucky, Gen. John M. Palmer, to apprehend or kill one man: William Clarke Quantrill.

On that May 10 morning, Terrell and his band were only a few miles from Quantrill. A tradesman had spotted Quantrill's gang as they rode past on the way to Wakefield's, and sent Terrell and his men off in the same direction.

When Quantrill reached Wakefield's farm, he and most of his men climbed into the barn hayloft and fell asleep. A few others remained below, playing cards or talking idly.

One of Quantrill's men happened to look up at the pasture slopes nearby. He saw men on horseback, unslinging their rifles, descending on the barn lot. He cried out a warning.

Quantrill and his companions in the loft scurried down, and some leaped onto horses stabled in the barn or tied up outside. As they fled, they fired their pistols at Terrell's men who were now upon them. Most of the Quantrill gang who were on horseback jumped a gate across their path and escaped through the orchard. The other men, whose horses were rearing at the noise and confusion, were unable to mount; so they ran from the barn and plunged into a pond. Submerged low in the water and hidden by rushes, they waited until their pursuers rode by in chase of the others.

Quantrill struggled to mount his new horse, but the animal was so frightened by the gunfire, and was rearing so wildly, that Quantrill was unable to get his boot into a stirrup, and could not haul himself up into the saddle. He decided to escape by foot, and called out for help as he raced toward the orchard. Two of his fleeing men, astride their horses, reined in and waited for Quantrill to reach them, firing all the while at his pursuers. But one of the horses was struck by rifle fire, and became uncontrollable. Quantrill fired his pistol at riders bearing down on him. He then turned toward the second horse, trying to pull himself up behind its rider.

Suddenly a bullet tore into his back, below the left shoulder blade, and descended downward, lodging against his spine. It paralyzed his body below the shoulders, and he dropped face down onto the ground.

A moment later, the two members of his gang who had tried to save him were shot and killed. The pursuers turned around, and came back to the wounded man lying prostrate on the ground. They stripped him of his boots, lifted his pistols out of their holsters, and went through his pockets. Among the articles they found was a picture of a young woman. Her identity was not known.

Quantrill was taken by wagon a few days later to a military prison's hospital in Louisville. A physician told him that his wound was fatal. His back had also been broken. Quantrill could speak, but he remained paralyzed. Reportedly, he made no effort to contact his mother or other family members, to tell them he was dying.

William Clarke Quantrill died in the late afternoon on June 6, 1865. He was twenty-seven years old. Civil conflict, culminating in the four years of Civil War, was at last at an end. The monstrous price paid was the loss of more American lives in battle during those four years than all other battle deaths in subsequent wars through present times.

Leah Gill Noland

After Marcus Gill and Mary Jane fled to Texas in April 1861, their oldest daughter, Leah, returned to the village of New Santa Fe from Independence. She was pregnant with her first child, conceived before her husband, Jesse, left for the South to join the Confederate Army.

In late January 1862, nine months into the war, Leah became apprehensive about skirmishes being fought near New Santa Fe. Her baby was due within days. Feeling endangered, she realized that she needed the care and support of her husband's family. So she decided to leave New Santa Fe for Independence, sixteen miles away.

Leah chose to make the journey after dark, hoping that she would be able to avoid exposure to any fighting. With the aid of a Negro girl, she hitched a yoke of oxen to a wagon, loaded the few articles she would need, and set out with the girl sharing the wagon seat beside her. It was a wintry night; flames from houses and barns burning in the countryside lighted the way.

Driving the slow-moving oxen throughout the night, and following less-traveled country roads, it was not until early morning that they reached the outskirts of Independence. Suddenly, they were confronted by a patrol of Union soldiers. Looking for known Confederate sympathizers, the armed cavalrymen demanded to know where her father and brothers, and the men in her husband's family, could be found. Leah replied that they were no longer in Jackson County.

Angered, because they felt that she was simply refusing to disclose the actual whereabouts of her family, the soldiers led her to a nearby house where the unit's commander was located. Again Leah was asked to tell them where the men in the family could be found. Stubbornly, she insisted that she did not know. Two of the soldiers, infuriated by her refusal to cooperate, seized her by the arms and dragged her into a nearby room where they locked her up with the Negro girl.

Soon after, Leah began giving birth, possibly a result of the rough, night-long journey on the ox-drawn wagon to Independence. The unit commander sent for a doctor. Leah gave birth to a boy whom she named Jesse Price Noland, after the popular Missouri Confederate leader, Gen. Sterling Price. Several days later, Leah was taken to a jail in Independence, but was soon paroled on the condition that she leave the area. She was handed a pass through the Union lines.

With little money, Leah set out for Texas with her infant son. They went alone, by ox-drawn wagon, with few provisions. Of necessity, she foraged off the country. Meanwhile, Jesse Noland had surrendered in the fighting at Vicksburg, and set free under the proviso that he not participate in the fighting again; so he himself was on his way to Texas.

It was more than twenty years later that Leah's father, Marcus Gill, divided up ownership of his farm among his eight surviving children. Leah was the only one excluded from the distribution; only speculation can devise a reason. Two years later, Leah divorced her husband, Jesse Noland, with whom she had borne nine children during their twenty-five years of marriage.

The following year, in 1886, Marcus Gill at age seventy-two addressed a letter to the husband of the oldest of his married daughters, Susan Gill McGee. From his and Mary

Jane's new home near Plattsburg, Missouri, Marcus wrote:

> We (received) a letter of Leah. We will send it to you. Take care of it and send it back after my children read it as I don't think we will answer it. There is no sense in it.

Leah later remarried and relocated to Colorado Springs, Colorado. She lived there for some years, but died in Ogden, Utah, in 1908, at age sixty-four.

Enoch Bruton Gill

Soon after Marcus Gill and Mary Jane arrived in Fayette County, Texas, with Turner and their younger children in May 1861, Enoch and Turner enlisted in the fledgling Confederate Army. Enoch was twenty-two when he enlisted, Turner only twenty. Enoch fought in battles in Mississippi, where he was wounded a year later. The injury caused the amputation of one leg, below the knee. Released from military service, he returned to his home in Texas and taught school for the remainder of the war.

In 1866 Enoch and his wife left Texas and settled in Clay County, Missouri, across the Missouri River from Kansas City, where he again taught school. He began the study of law, and was admitted to the Missouri Bar in 1871, at age thirty-two. He practiced law for fifteen years, but in 1886, at age forty-seven, he began giving full time to a farm he owned near Olathe in Johnson County, Kansas, where he became known for the fine quality of farm animals he bred and raised.

Enoch died in 1916 at age seventy-six, and is buried in Elmwood Cemetery in Kansas City, Missouri, with his second wife, who lived until 1932.

Turner Anderson Gill

Turner Anderson Gill, like Enoch, was also in the midst of the fighting in Mississippi. Promoted to the rank of lieutenant in Company A, 6th Missouri Infantry, he fought at Vicksburg, where he was taken prisoner by Union forces. In the fall of 1863, Turner was included in an exchange of prisoners. He was immediately assigned as adjutant in the 2nd Missouri Cavalry. Not long afterward, at the age of twenty-three, he was promoted by Gen. Jo Shelby "for merit and gallantry under fire" to the rank of captain of the same unit in which he was then serving.

When the war ended, Turner Gill studied law at Kentucky University, graduating with honors in 1868. He was admitted to the Missouri Bar and opened an office in Kansas City. For a time, Turner Gill was a partner in a law firm whose successor firm is today known as Lathrop & Gage, one of the several largest law firms in Kansas City. A photographic portrait of him is displayed in the firm's office. In 1875 Turner Gill was elected mayor of Kansas City, Missouri, and re-elected for a second term in 1876. When he left office, he later served as City Counselor.

In 1881, at age forty, Turner Gill was appointed a judge of the circuit court; elected to the same position in 1882; and re-elected in 1886. Two years later, in 1888, as the Democratic candidate for judge of the U.S. Court of Appeals, Western District, he was elected by a wide margin and served in this position for thirteen years, until 1901.

Turner Anderson Gill died in 1919 at age seventy-seven and is buried in the Gill family burial plot in Elmwood Cemetery. Marcus Gill, Mary Jane Gill, and other family members are also there.

Sources

Barton, O. S. *Three Years With Quantrill. A True Story Told by His Scout, John McCorkle.* Norman: University of Oklahoma Press, (1914) 1992.

Castel, Albert, "The Bloodiest Man in American History," in *Kansas Revisited: Historical Images and Perspectives.* Ed. by Paul K. Stuewe. Lawrence: University of Kansas, 1990.

Christopher, Sue Hargis. *My Mother's Families (Paternal): Gill, Malone, and Duncan.* Kansas City, Mo., 1953.

Connelley, William E. *Quantrill and the Border Wars.* Ottawa: Kansas Heritage Press, (1910) 1992.

Farley, Alan W. "When Lincoln Came to Kansas Territory." Address to the Fort Leavenworth (Kans.) Historical Society, 17 November 1959.

———"Abraham Lincoln in Kansas Territory: December 1 to 7, 1859." Fort Leavenworth, Kans., n.d.

Fellman, Michael. *Inside War: The Guerrilla Conflict in Missouri During the American Civil War.* New York: Oxford University Press, 1989.

Gerlach, Russell L. *Settlement Patterns in Missouri: A Study of Population Origins.* Columbia: University of Missouri Press, 1986.

Gill, Thos F. *History of the Gill Family.* Hannibal, Mo.: Standard Printing Co., 1893.

Hale, Donald R. *We Rode with Quantrill: Quantrill and the Guerrilla War as Told by the Men and Women Who Were With Him, with a True Sketch of Quantrill's Life.* Lees Summit, Mo.: n.p., 1974, 1992.

Leslie, Edward E. *The Devil Knows How to Ride: The True Story of William Clarke Quantrill and His Confederate Raiders.* New York: Random House, 1996.

Nelson, Earl J. "Missouri Slavery:1861-1865." *Missouri Historical Review,* 28 (July 1934).

Paludan, Philip Shaw. "The Meaning of the Civil War." Lecture, University of Kansas, Lawrence, May 28, 1993.

Paludan, Phillip Shaw. *The Presidency of Abraham Lincoln.* Lawrence: University Press of Kansas, 1994.

"Quantrill Letters." Kansas Collection, Kenneth L. Spencer Memorial Library, University of Kansas, Lawrence.

Sheridan, Richard. "Victims and Consequences." Lecture, University of Kansas, Lawrence, May 27, 1993.